"MA! MA . . . MA . . . MA . . . MA!
IT WAS A CRY THAT VERGED
ON HYSTERIA. . . .

Alison raced toward the front of the house and caught Maud who was racing toward her. The little girl's face was white and filled with terror. Alison knew immediately what had happened. She took the pile of postcards from the child's hands and gasped.

There was a woman . . . at least Alison thought that's what it was . . . a face, framed with soft, brown hair, the fine ends blending into a dark, glossy stain on the pillow beneath. A hand lay severed from its arm. Alison felt her eyes glaze over, her stomach heave.

"My God!" she cried. "Who's doing this to me?"

Wish You Were Here

HARRIET STEINBERG

PUBLISHED BY POCKET BOOKS NEW YORK

Another *Original* publication of POCKET BOOKS

POCKET BOOKS, a division of Simon & Schuster, Inc.
1230 Avenue of the Americas, New York, N.Y. 10020

ISBN: 0-671-61980-2

First Pocket Books printing April 1987

10 9 8 7 6 5 4 3 2 1

POCKET and colophon are registered trademarks of Simon & Schuster, Inc.

Printed in the U.S.A.

To my father, the late Dr. Charles S. Steinberg, whose brilliance, integrity, and trust inspired me to begin writing.

To my mother, Hortense Steinberg, who achieved the impossible and filled his shoes and whose unending faith, love, and support has kept me writing.

To my husband, Tom Zafian, who always believed in me even when I didn't.

And to Susie, Tangerine, Ziggy, Wilford, and Ardie for loving me back.

This book is dedicated to you all, with my love and thanks.

Chapter 1

WHACK!
      The blade split the pillow, falling just a breath from its target as she turned her sleeping face, suddenly showered with feathers; a lock of severed hair.

Then, her scream.

That scream filled his head and echoed as he jammed his fists over his ears, hunched in the hard-backed, regulation chair, face buried in his knees. Slowly, a stiff, convulsive movement in his right arm passed in ripples across his back and faded as his eyes caught a glimpse of approaching white shoes and the squeak of rubber soles on the linoleum penetrated the scream in his head.

Shoes, white-stockinged legs a bit on the heavy side, a white skirt hem, ample hips, full bustline tugging at its bindings, and that face—starched, papery-thin skin stretched tight just like the uniform and brown, forgettable hair. His eyes traveled upward over this familiar figure to find an unfamiliar expression—she was smiling at him.

"Good news, Mr. Smith. The doctors have decided you're well enough to go home."

Alden Smith sat opposite the worn, dark-wood desk and waited. He was very good at waiting. His hands lay motionless in his lap, legs slightly apart and feet flat on the floor. His head was bowed just enough to imply deference but not disinterest. Sunlight caught the edges of the steel mesh that covered the large window behind the desk, mesh not nearly as obvious as bars but just as intimidating. An errant ray caught the tip of the bright red second hand on the round, white-faced wall clock and focused Alden's attention. For a full minute he watched it as the click, click, click of a ticking timepiece in his brain replaced the silent circle of the electric arm.

"Mr. Smith?"

The words broke the pattern of ticking just as it had begun to soothe him. He looked at the clock for a last three seconds until the hand was even on a number, then swung his gaze slowly to meet the eyes of the man seated opposite him.

"Mr. Smith, we feel you've shown marvelous improvement since you've been with us. Just spectacular!" The man waited for a reply from Alden, settled at last for the deadpan stare of seeming attention, and went on, raising his enthusiasm an octave to compensate for Alden's silence. "In fact, the doctors who've evaluated your case file"—here he began a steady, arrhythmic tapping on the neat manila folder in his left hand, using a very sharp pencil—"feel you're quite well. Here, let me read you a small section . . ." The man looked up at Alden in anticipation of an excited reaction to this most unprecedented of gifts and fought off a nervous twitching that crept upon his left shoulder when he was greeted with glassy patience instead. "Here," he repeated grudgingly, now reluctant to follow through with his offer, "let's see now." He was playing a game with Alden, trading action for reaction and getting stiffed by the opposition. He didn't like it when his game turned out this way. Just who was this Mr. Smith to change the rules?

"Ah, yes . . ." He opened, seemingly at random, to the middle of the file, and read aloud. "Mr. Smith, in

8

our opinion, shows a remarkable preparedness for functional normalcy in the world outside the institution . . . ." He served this tidbit to Alden as a tidy appetizer, intimating that there was more for the asking but reluctantly realizing that he was not going to be asked. Directness, he thought, would perhaps revive this cold fish.

"This"—he punctuated his remarks with more taps on the folder—"is your file. A file we're about to close." He put the pencil down and held the file out just beyond Alden's reach. Alden remained still. "Aren't you pleased? Don't you have something to say to us?" The man scolded himself silently for having given in—for letting this other man get to him. This was not at all part of the game. It was still his playing field, his rule book, and the control must remain his. Grudgingly, he chalked up a few points in Alden's column. Perhaps he was one of the rare few who was aware of this private contest at all. The man glanced over Alden's shoulder to the starched nurse who shadowed the patient from about three feet behind. A brief, reflexive smile passed over Alden's thin lips. The man behind the desk grabbed at it and went on, using that smile as tacit agreement that, indeed, this file was closed. He chalked up a couple of points in his column. He was enjoying the challenge of this match.

"Well, then. Let's get right down to details," he said, planting both hands firmly on the desk and locking into Alden's gaze. "Here"—he offered a slip of paper—"is a prescription for your medicine. It is *very* important that you maintain vigilance and keep taking your pills. You know we've all grown fond of you, Mr. Smith, but just the same, we won't be holding your bed!" A jaundiced smile flashed on the man's face. Alden returned the smile, reached for the piece of paper, and folded it very meticulously into three parts before placing it on his knee and covering it exactly with his left hand.

"Don't you think you'd better put that away?" the nurse piped in, sternly. Alden tilted his head just a fraction in her direction but did not try to catch her eye. "That's quite all right, Miss Brigham, I know just what Mr. Smith is thinking," the man said, and pulled a heavy canvas duffel bag from beneath his desk. He hoisted it up to rest on the surface and waited calculatedly for Alden to react. After a moment of silence the man went on, letting his own enthusiasm fend for itself in the atmosphere of Alden's unconcern. Quickly he began pulling objects from the bag as he talked.

"Look here, Mr. Smith. All your things are just as they were when you . . . er . . . left them in our custody. Here." He handed Alden a worn brown wallet. "Why don't you put that prescription away where it will be safe?"

Alden took the wallet, held it for a second, stuffed the paper inside, and put the leather case into the breast pocket of his jacket.

Not satisfied, the man went on. "You'll notice, Mr. Smith, that we've taken *good* care of you," he hinted, then, not getting the desired reaction, crossed from behind the desk to beside Alden and reached into his breast pocket. Inside the wallet, he made sure to show Alden, were bright, new bills—one hundred of them. "We know you came to us with a bit less but we felt you should have a fresh, new start in every way!" Again, mustard teeth revealed themselves. Alden returned the smile—an action as disconnected as the reflexive movement of a spider's legs after its body has been squashed.

The man bridled a bit at this mild response, adopting a more formal, less paternal tone as he returned to his side of the desk. "We've taken the liberty, as we often do for our 'graduates,' of arranging with the proper authorities for you to be provided with a regular stipend until you get back on your feet. You see, we know how hard it can be to find work in this economy, especially, with your particular references"—he could not refrain from a mild chuckle—"but we want you to know that we believe in you and that we here have total faith in your ability to rejoin the mainstream just as soon as possible." He fought an urge to rise and wave his right hand in the air with impassioned patriotism. Wasn't it a magnificent country that had a social welfare system ready and waiting to provide a fresh start for the Alden Smiths of America, to carry on the dedicated work of institutions such as this one. . . . He let his enthusiasm wane as Alden's deadpan brought him back to the issue at hand.

"Well then, all you'll have to do is fill in the rest of these forms with your new address and the checks should begin arriving in just a few weeks." He extended two half-completed forms hesitantly, knowing Alden would not meet him halfway, withdrew his arm and slid the papers into the duffel bag. He rested his arm on top of the green canvas and resumed his tapping, now muffled, on its soft surface. "You'll find that all your things are here, just as I said." Picking away at Alden for some kind of reply, he continued, "Would you care to double-check us on that?" The man offered the bag to Alden. "Well!" upon getting no response. "That's all right. If anything is missing, you know where to find us!" The man burst into laughter as much to relieve his own discomfort as to cut the mood in the room and Miss Brigham, on cue, joined in.

Tinny, irregular sounds invaded Alden's head and he winced as the laughter penetrated deeper. A slow crescendo began and then the reverberation took over and boomed inside him. Swelling, receding, swelling, receding like kettledrums pounding, the laughter attacked—then stopped. They were watching him. Subtly, Alden released the tight fist he had begun to form with his right hand and watched the knuckles turn back from white to pink. The man behind the desk stood up and extended his right hand. Alden followed, mimicking his every move to get it right, as he had done so often in his childhood and, later, in what they

11

called the dormant years of his illness. The chair slid back, just so, and Alden stood. His proffered hand met the man's and they shook. He noted last-minute instructions to check in every six weeks, let them know his new address and telephone, remember to file the papers with the welfare department so he would get his checks, let them know if he needed any help. And *don't* forget the pills. A bottle with a two-week supply of the drug found its way into Alden's palm and he slipped it into his pocket. The man watched, smiling, as Miss Brigham led Alden to the office door, its small glass window covered, too, with steel mesh, and out into the corridor. The door edged closed as the smile faded from the man's face. On his desk, a slim, manila folder with the name Alden Smith on its flap lay separate from the piles of other papers. The man picked it up and weighed it lightly in his hand for a moment before slipping it into a square plastic basket on the upper-right-hand corner of the desk. On the front of the basket, neatly lettered, the word *out*.

Miss Brigham guided Alden to the end of the hall, around curves and through gates and stiles he hadn't been near in over four years. Her left hand dragged his bag while with her right she manipulated a ring laden with dozens of keys. Soon, the last gate, the final padlock, opened.

"Well, Alden, it's time to say goodbye," she offered him her hand which he took hesitantly and dropped instantly. Miss Brigham shook her head in puzzlement at this man who, after four years of care at her hands, could still not accept her touch in peace. She opened the front door wide and sunlight bounded in, startling the dreary halls and gray entryway. Alden shut his eyes and swayed in its intensity. Miss Brigham smiled.

"You'll get used to that pretty quick, Alden, I can promise you that. . . . Well." Her voice nudged him closer to the threshold. "Goodbye, Mr. Smith." Alden took the bag she handed him and awkwardly slung its weight over his shoulder, tottered at the imbalance, and compensated by hitching his burdened side up a few inches. He tugged at his pants just slightly and felt them slide back down to his hips.

Everything hung on him now and it seemed that even his shoulders had shrunk in that place—the sleeves on his faded tweed jacket were at least an inch too long. He took a step out the door and stood a moment, precariously, before bidding his other foot to follow. A second later he remembered Miss Brigham and turned to say goodbye. The door closed behind him with a deafening slam. He paused, staring at the door, half expecting it to reopen and welcome him back, tell him it was all a mistake. A sense of discomfort, an uncleanliness crept upon him and he glanced down at the source, shivered, and shifted his duffel bag to the other shoulder in order to rub the offending hand furiously against his trousers, to wipe off Miss Brigham's unwelcome touch. He looked about him with caution, sensing her watchful eye, but he was alone. He turned from the door.

The sunlight still threatened his unaccustomed eyes and he cowered before it, reluctant to venture beyond the first step. "Mr. Alden Smith?" The voice belonged to a young man in orderly's whites. "Mr. Smith?" the voice insisted. Alden looked down the steps at the man. "Come with me, I'll see you get out the gate."

A few moments later Alden found himself on the sidewalk in front of the ten-foot iron fence that surrounded his recent home. Across the street a bus stop sign beckoned him and he reluctantly crossed to meet it. "Good day," a stranger said as Alden passed.

The bus was nearly empty and Alden had a double window seat all to himself. A light breeze filtered through the window and turned cooler and softer as the bus neared the shore. Alden pushed the window open all the way and rested his elbow on the ridged ledge, his chin on his hand. His thoughts wandered, gently led by that ocean scent and he flashed briefly on

13

memories brought back by that wonderful smell. A just-steamed lobster on a plate surrounded by rice and tomatoes; a castle in the sand, half washed away by a brutal surf; a volleyball game on the sand—his sun-tanned fist striking savagely at the ball; a carpeted staircase somewhere in a dark house, late at night; a small child's doll resting aslant in a miniature rocking chair. . . .

Outside the window familiar sights brought Alden back to the present. A delicate, wood-frame church, newly painted white and a solid brick schoolhouse with a basketball court to one side and sprawling green playing fields beyond. Hot, shiny streaks on the sweating asphalt beneath the bus's wheels and a stream of quickly warming water running from the mouth of a roadside fire hydrant. A burned-out building—gaping staircase obscenely revealed to passersby.

A sudden flash to the dark, carpeted, midnight staircase in that somewhere house; the child's doll now lying broken four steps from the top; a flash of white sheets, a paisley wall, pink bedspread—splattered with blood and chips of bone; young, nightgowned child—gashed—blood dripping on the carpeted, dark night stairs. The bus jerked to a stop sending Alden into the railing on the seat in front of him.

"Last stop. Oceanview. Last stop." The driver was talking to him. Alden wiped a drizzle of sweat from the bridge of his nose. He took his bag and climbed off the bus.

It was hot at the beach and Alden stopped to remove his jacket, looking around at the familiar beachfront stores and rooming houses. One old, ramshackle wood structure caught his eye and he focused on the "Rooms to Let" sign in front. Making that his destination, he headed across the sandy concrete sidewalk, dragging his bag behind him in a lazy, zigzag pattern and counting his steps meticulously to avoid intrusive thoughts. He climbed the steps awkwardly, letting the bag bump behind him, and pushed the screen door open.

The man at the desk inside eyed Alden cautiously for a minute or two before rising from his stool and approaching the counter. A double row of empty mailboxes, many with keys inside, decorated the wall behind him and the lobby smelled of seaweed and mildew. He watched Alden again, waiting for some word or sign, and then, finally, said, "You want a room or what?"

No answer.

Then, "Eight dollars a night. Two nights in advance. Two dollars extra for private bath," the man said. Alden walked closer, stood for a minute, and then pulled his wallet from his jacket but made no move to remove any money. Exasperated, the man took the wallet from Alden's limp hand, looked at Alden closely. "Yep, you want a private bath," counted out twenty dollars and handed the wallet back. Turning, he grabbed a key from one of the mailboxes, stuffed it in Alden's hand, and said, "Room twelve, up the stairs, corner, in the back," and watched Alden slowly follow his directions. "Summer people!" he said in disgust, and shook his head.

Upstairs Alden had no trouble finding the corner room assigned to him. It was dark and acrid-smelling inside, and Alden waited in the hall awhile before venturing in. Once beyond the door he quickly took stock of the room, cataloging the scant furniture and noting the size, depth, and placement of objects in the room. With each glance he lined up a shot—meticulously measuring every frame, faintly pleased at the returning awareness of his passions without being conscious of either the pleasure or the source. A single bed covered with a boldly flowered spread was the focal point of the place. An old dresser and scratched mirror also caught the eye. There was one window which hadn't been opened, it seemed, in years, and a torn screen. Alden's innate sense of order missed the second window a corner room should have had and, in its place, he noted a washroom door. A faded imitation Oriental rug covered the center of the floor and a bridge table served as a desk with an old, folding chair and brass lamp the only accessories. There was a night table as well, equipped with a cracked, glass-based lamp, the yellow bulb in which had long since burned out, and a faded copy of Gideon's Bible.

On the far wall a vase of yellow flowers sat off center on a round table in a crudely framed painting, annoying his need for symmetry, and Alden's first motion in his new home was to remove it and slide it behind the bureau. The neat, properly spaced stain mark left by the old picture frame on the faded wallpaper filled Alden with an appropriate sense of calm and he gazed at it almost lovingly as if it represented a personal bond between him and this new home.

He let his eyes drift from the stain to examine the room thoroughly before venturing further and his narrow, focused vision picked out each object, framed it, clicked, and filed the image away in his head. He approached the bed, tested it with his palm, and placed his duffel bag on the foot. Then he went over to the bathroom, flicked on the light, and began checking the tub, sink, and toilet water by letting everything run at once. A gloppy, brown fluid vomited from the faucets, fading to yellow in a few seconds. Eventually the water ran clear and Alden stuck his face under the nozzle in the sink and let the water run over him. A moment later he stood up, dripping, and groped for the towel rack—empty. "Fuck!" Alden said, and grabbed some toilet paper to dry his face.

Towels, he later learned, were stuck in the bottom drawer of the dresser—yellow, mildewed things that made him glad he'd found the toilet paper before them. He sat on the bed and dumped the contents of his bag in front of him, viewing these things for the first time in years. Jockey shorts, Ts, socks, a pair of chinos, a few clean shirts, a terry robe, sneakers, a toothbrush, a comb, a hand mirror, a Timex watch, a notebook filled with framed sketches like tiny photographs, a small pocket knife, keys (to what he didn't recall), faded handkerchiefs, dark sunglasses (how he wished he'd had these earlier), and, last to fall from the bag, a huge case full of photographic equipment—three expensive cameras, lenses, light meters, a tripod, automatic advance attachment, bulk film loader, developing equipment, telephoto lens, and much, much more. He picked up each piece as a child with a new toy— touching, caressing, squeezing, and fondling every shutter, button, and switch. An hour passed, then another while Alden examined and played with every item. It grew late and Alden finally strapped a leather thong to one camera and wrapped it around his body. It settled immediately into a familiar groove and Alden felt calm—reunited with an appendage he had long missed but avoided thinking about. Leaving everything else in a jumble on his bed, he took the key from the bureau and left the room.

There had been no film in the bag, not even a finished snapshot, and Alden's first thought was to buy some. Seeing a drugstore he walked toward it, entered, and spent nearly forty dollars on film and supplies. He wasn't quite sure why he bought the developing fluid, solutions, and other products except that the action was reflexive. It had been quite some time since Alden had developed a photograph and, quite frankly, he wasn't sure he still could. Anyway, he had everything he needed to try and so left the store and began to walk down the street toward the residential part of town. His camera still empty, he enjoyed the feel of that bulge at his ribs and barely felt the bulk of the brown bag full of accessories. He walked on, his brain clicking away at images and objects in his path.

The drugstore stood near the center of a long line of small shops and businesses that included the regulation pizza parlor, ice cream store, supermarket, toy shop, liquor emporium, shoemaker, tailor, bakery, card store, deli, and numerous tiny boutiques catering each to one version of a single specialty—women's budget fashions. A few minutes' walk down the street, the row of commercial buildings gave way to a quiet beach community that ritually boomed in summer and lay near-dormant the other nine months of the year. Permanent residents often rented their homes to transients for the busy season and took off for Europe or Florida. Most of the people in town now were city types who took a beach house for a few weeks to let their kids breathe. Few came from more than a couple of hours' drive away.

One of the last buildings on the strip was a large, Colonial-style bank that Alden recognized immediately. An image of a blue bankbook, opened to a white page with black, typed letters spelling out *Alden Smith* and the amount—"$10,000"—passed before his eyes and faded as he looked up at the bank. He blinked, remembered the sunglasses he had left on his bed, and walked on. Suddenly, from beyond the bank the sound of giggles—the high-pitched, silly sounds of children— filtered toward him. A blue frisbee whooshed through the air beside his head followed by a breathless youngster in cutoffs and high-top sneakers. A heavy shield began to close in his brain and his peripheral vision left him. He tried to shut his ears too, began counting his steps quickly—two numbers to each step. But the sound kept jabbing away at him, finally piercing through to his brain and pricking him, making him squirm and tremble and seethe. His right hand slowly formed itself into a tight fist and began to pound harder and harder on his thigh, the knuckles turning white as the skin tightened and stretched thin.

Another image came—brief, hot, and fleeting—a child, blood dripping from a huge gash in her face, cowering in a corner; her life fluid streaked brown-red on the wall behind her. Gone. He walked faster, his hand pounding, pounding at his leg, the whole fist white, his eyes blank, his face taut and ghostly. A middle-aged couple coming toward him and he, heading straight into them. "Jeez!" a male voice, furious. "What institution did they let you out from?" He walked on, unnoticing, as they looked at each other and quickened their pace in the opposite direction.

A second later he slowed, paused to gaze blankly after them, and then, slowly, slowly creeping upon him, a smile. He felt it trigger a metamorphosis, his blood turning into a numbing, icy liquid that calmed and tempered his pulse, relaxed his muscles, and loosened his fist. He shivered. The sensation left him and he resumed his slow, patternless wandering past several small streets lined with cottages framed with tidy lawns and uniform shrubbery. That smile, though, still haunted his lips as they moved ever so slightly in an unheard chant that emanated from deep within him. "Children must be seen and not heard, not heard, never heard . . ." And his thin lips danced over and over these words as he walked on, heading blindly toward the quiet of the beach.

It was nearly suppertime and there were few people on the streets. An occasional car passed him, turned into a driveway, and emitted a shirt-sleeved, open-collared man with briefcase in hand and jacket over his arm. Children ran out to meet one of these men and Alden quickly turned a corner and found himself heading toward the sand as he raised up the volume of the chant in his head and speeded his pace.

At the sand's edge a row of concessions, restrooms, and water fountains greeted him. A few late sunbathers lay on the sand in the late-afternoon sun. Alden walked along the strip of sidewalk nearest to the beach until he reached the steps leading up to the boardwalk. Climbing slowly, his mind clicked at a swarm of termites dining on the rotting wood, focused on a loose board and a sign warning people to stay away from that section. He moved on.

The boardwalk ran the length of the poorer section

of the town. Its side was lined with cottages whose yards opened right onto the sand, and the smell of barbecues wafted over him. A few blocks down, a bright orange building stood out from the surrounding white-board buildings that flanked it. A sign, painted in huge black letters, announced *"Fotofast,"* and Alden stared at it in sudden panic, his hand convulsively fighting its way back into a fist.

A barrage of images tumbled at him: plates of developing fluid; a man's hands delicately soaking a print in liquid; the click, click, clicking of a camera shutter. His head became a camera, his eyes the lens, and memories snapped past him. Stifling the torrent of pictures, he walked on, this time with a destination clearly before him and a determined swing to his walk. His camera bounced against his chest and his fist relaxed at his side.

Ten minutes' walk from the first *Fotofast* another one presented itself to Alden. This time it was located on an island in the middle of a two-way, multilane road which led to the better part of town. Alden stepped off the curb, watched the light turn red, and stepped back, his brain clicking along with the "don't walk" sign that flashed at him. The light changed and he crossed to the orange shack, stopping to stare at the boarded window, the padlock on the door. A sign on the window read: *"Fotofast* has moved to . . ."

Alden stayed in front of the building for a while, watching it for signs of life. In a moment of decisiveness he picked up a rock and quickly smashed the flimsy padlock, stuffed it in his pocket, and slipped inside the door. The place was just as he recalled—rusted now, and crawling with roaches and mice but still nearly intact. He traced the counter with his finger, blew off some dust, and made his way to the back. Tables, sinks, and shelves met his eyes and he watched from the doorway that led to the old darkroom, reluctant to disturb its memories with his presence. A few posters remained on the walls, now yellow with age and moisture but still beautiful in his eyes. That one, there, he recalled, he had printed himself—a black-and-white study of a pigeon sitting on the edge of the boardwalk during a rainstorm. He reached up and pushed back the flaking, curled edge of the poster, admiring the subtle variations in light and clouds his camera had captured. He let himself settle into a pleasant reverie and breathed in the stale, musty sea air in the place.

He watched a gray mouse nibble at some invisible bit of sustenance and scurry off behind a shelf. He edged his way into the room and felt the sinks, the table, the edge of the sign at the door that said *"In Use."* The glass over the sign had long since been broken, but Alden flipped the switch anyway, hoping that it would light up for him. Of course, he told himself, they've shut off the current. And the water too, he mused as he played with a faucet on the deep, white sink. Memory conjured smells of pungent chemicals, stale coffee, and late-night sweat. Touch brought life back to the cobwebbed room at his fingertips.

A horn sounded on the road outside and Alden was dragged back to the present. Turning to leave the darkroom, he picked up on a dark, hand-lettered sign off to his left that read *"Men."* Suddenly he knew why he had come there, why he had stood and waited so long in the damp, unpleasant air, why he had felt so much a part of this place where he had worked years earlier. A part of him was still here—a part rooted in the firmest reality, hidden behind the walls of that rest room. He turned his steps in the direction of the sign and opened the bathroom door.

It was a very small room, equipped only with a pull-chain toilet and tiny sink. The walls were coming apart, having been built of flimsy plywood, and a single, small window let a strand of light in through a jagged hole in its murky glass. Alden went to work immediately, tearing at the strips of shingled wood that formed the walls and tossing them haphazardly behind

21

him. Soon he reached his goal and began removing the wood more carefully as the items hidden behind it became visible. The first few panels came off easily and it was with no emotion that Alden reached behind them and drew out handfuls of moldy, motheaten, but still whole bills. Without glancing at the wads of tens and twenties, he threw the cash—many thousands of dollars—onto the floor. Stripping the walls of the last pieces of old wood until he had uncovered the real goal of his mission—some four hundred three-by-five-inch color photographs beneath, most carefully preserved from mildew by the blanket of Alden's life savings.

Moisture had reached only a few of the photos and he carefully examined each one, more for water damage than content, as he piled them one after the other on the cover of the john, stopping only occasionally to click off an internal comment on a particular shot. A rare hint of a smile, a soft clicking of the tongue, were his only comments until, pausing over one simple shot of the beautiful woman who was his wife, an involuntary grunt escaped his lips. He jumped, looking nervously around for the source of the sound, unused to anything but his own controlled bodily silence. Yes, it was he who had made that sound; he was still quite alone. He let his shoulders relax again as he resumed gathering the photos together. Sifting gently through the pile, he was drawn inexplicably back to his wife's image and drew it out toward him, holding it up to catch a ray of light from the bathroom window. It had not changed. There was still that imbalance—the imperfection of the human face, the slightly off-center lines and irregular curves that defiled the flawlessness of the artist's lens. Even he, in whose hands a camera could once perform miracles, was powerless against those defiant human flaws.

Angrily, he swept the neat pile of photographs off the john onto the floor, sending them skittering to all corners of the tiny washroom. Suddenly remorseful, he sprawled over the floor trying to somehow protect the photos from his fury. No, they were not injured, and he gratefully swept them toward him in soft strokes, simultaneously taking up a soft, steady mental count, "one, two, three, four, five . . . one, two, three, four, five . . ." to anesthetize himself, to wipe out the deadly anger that had fatally disturbed the symmetry once before.

One by one he restacked the photos on top of the toilet lid, gazing with passionless eyes over pictures of his wife; then of their two young daughters; then gathering whole groups of photos, image upon image, until they blended together in a homogeneous mass. Only the occasional stark shot stood out—a child's doll, a delicate hand, a strange grouping of shots of a carpet and staircase, oddly blotched with what appeared to be dark coffee stains.

True, she who had, for Alden, embodied perfection beyond the infallible eye of the lens, had betrayed him by stepping before it. But in using his camera to correct her wrongs, he realized, he had betrayed himself. To restore symmetry where it never was and put balance and order in the place of disarray had been a madman's task, but to attempt it all with the sacred tools that had created the error in the first place was the act of a fool.

A sudden wave of sadness blanketed the frustration and despair memory had foisted upon him, and he gathered up the rest of the photos without even glancing at them or thinking about what their price had been. Perhaps, he allowed himself to enjoy the thought for just a moment, he would one day restore the symmetry.

It suddenly became important to him to hurry his work and he stacked the photos quickly and put them in the brown paper bag with his film and equipment. As an afterthought, he gathered up the cash from the floor and stuffed it in the bag, his trousers and shirt, and everywhere else he could fit the bundles of bills and left without looking back.

Outside again, Alden meticulously replaced the broken padlock, gave a last look at the dilapidated structure, and took a cautious glance around him to see if he had been observed. The neighborhood was quiet. Alden crossed the street, retraced his steps almost exactly to the edge of the boardwalk, and turned toward home.

Chapter 2

IT was late in the day toward the end of that first week and the sun was beginning to glow with that sharp brightness just before setting. The glare forced Alden to shield his eyes while focusing his camera on the four people frolicking in the ocean a few blocks in the distance. The elbow formed by the wood railing at the end of the boardwalk offered a perfect niche for his arms, and he felt comfortable standing there, watching the sea rise and fall while casually noting the movement of the groups in the surf.

There! At last they were coming out of the water. Alden held the camera up to his face and focused.

Long strides brought the four closer to the house and the outdoor, cold water shower that rinsed the sand from them before going inside.

A minute turn of the focus brought them clearly into view and whiteness crept slowly upon Alden's right hand, inching into a tight, bony fist.

A quick rubdown with big, white terry towels and the family disappeared into the rear door of the house.

His hand relaxing just slightly, Alden panned the camera over the beach and back to the house, clicking off shots in his head as the camera paused to frame the back door, porch, picket fence, driveway, plastic garbage cans, green station wagon, and a sliver of the front street. The camera now resting in its cradle on

25

his chest, his right hand fell to his side and he began a slow weave in the opposite direction, down the boardwalk. Perhaps the symmetry would be restored.

James Sommers stepped out onto the veranda and surveyed the late-afternoon ocean thinking about the changes this summer had brought as his daughters' ideas of privacy, space, and personal boundaries expanded. Suddenly, there was ten-year-old Maud worrying about her tan and thirteen-year-old Beth panicking over an extra quarter ounce of fat on her upper thighs. Today it was Beth's obsessive exercising—strenuous calisthenics on the sand—that had set Maud off.

For the first time, James worried about keeping the peace when the family returned home from summer vacation in just a few days and the two girls found themselves, once more, sharing a bedroom that, until this year (and the luxury of separate rooms in the summer cottage) had been more than ample enough for their often very distinct moods. Why, just two summers ago, Maud had begged Beth to share her summertime room at the cottage—a far cry from the neatly lettered, starkly foreboding *"Keep Out—Do not disturb"* sign that the younger girl now hung outside her very private bedroom.

James stood on the elevated back porch that hung over the sand and surveyed the near-empty beach dappled in spots by soda spills and dribbles of suntan oil, a rare piece of trash blowing in the evening breeze toward the very blue ocean. He breathed deeply and, resting his bare arms on the railing, pivoted his lean, muscular upper body slowly as his gaze measured the beach, ocean, nearly matching sky.

Less than a quarter of a mile down the sand the sharp right angle that ended the boardwalk also served as a boundary line between the low-income, transient-in-summer, boarded-up-in-winter homes and the year-round residences that were often rented but only very selectively. Even the sand seemed whiter in the better part of town, clearly so because the beach was plowed and combed thoroughly before the Memorial Day weekend and once weekly at night throughout the summer until Labor Day. The sand at the other, poorer end of the beach was piled sloppily into heaps under the boardwalk, housing empty beer bottles, cans, and other debris, not to mention the occasional vagrant who found shelter under the rotting boards and sustenance in someone's discarded picnic box.

The town existed comfortably under this arbitrary but distinct division in classes although there were unspoken rules. Visits by the wealthier summer folk to the shopping strip in the less fortunate part of the community were enthusiastically encouraged, for example, while the reverse was most severely frowned upon. Still, it was a well-established rumor that some of the biggest shots in the good part of town held the deeds of some of the corroded, crumbling beach hotels on whose initially sturdy foundations the small community had been built decades earlier.

The Sommers, fairly new to the area, had spent their first full summer there only three years earlier. Longtime residents of a neat, suburban village an hour's drive inland—chosen carefully for its highly rated school system—they had discovered Oceanview quite by accident when a friend left the local tabloid in their car one weekend. James's eye had caught an ad for a "homey, fully decorated, two-story home on the beach—utilities included, very reasonable" and he decided, on the sly, to check it out.

The house had been standing empty, he learned, for nearly a year. But as neighbors to both sides were new to the area and old-timers reluctant to answer questions, James let the fresh air, expansive view, and seemingly wall-to-wall windows entice him into a meeting with the landlord. Persuasive fellow, he, as

27

James had found his signature on a two-month lease before he knew it and was on the phone to his wife Alison telling her to pack the kids and everything else portable and be ready to try summer-homing it when he got back.

Equipped with modern appliances, two baths, and best of all, separate bedrooms for the children, it quickly became their summer dream home. Freshly painted and cleaned, the only hint of a previous owner lay in a series of faded, coffee-colored stains on the second-floor carpet and on the the staircase.

"I guess we should think about doing something different next summer. Travel somewhere; get away for a change," James spoke reluctantly, half hoping Alison would quell the ever-more-solid feeling that this summer idyll had seen better days.

"I don't know." Alison wrapped her arms around him from behind and rested her chin on his shoulder. Her tall, slender frame fit comfortably into his and the tip of her chin settled easily into the niche on his shoulder as she peered out over the darkening beach. "I like it here. Maybe one more summer wouldn't hurt. If Beth doesn't want to come, she can get a job as a camp counselor. She's old enough."

"It wouldn't be the same. You know how I feel about us all being together. That's why I took this place to begin with. And it's been good for us—terrific, in fact. I just think maybe it's run its course." James spoke without turning.

Alison sighed, his instinct about the place spreading slowly over her as so often happened when he felt strongly about something. But then, that had been Alison's doing in her subtle, determined effort to enshrine James in his role as head of the household and to ease the nagging insecurities that come with a marriage between a good-looking but average man and an exceptionally beautiful, highly successful fashion model. Even her nine-year status as "ex" in the modeling category had done little to diminish the shadow she cast over him. Supporting him through most of his college years and a Master's degree in fine arts and earning three zeros more than he did even in a good year hadn't helped, though since then her every penny had been tucked away in stocks and bonds, the income from which was never spoken of or used for family expenses. It had been hard, and still was at times, to downplay her own ego and achievements in deference to his but then Alison's own mother had failed to do so in her marriage and had lost it. Alison was not about to let that happen to her.

And then, there was that smashing face of hers that stopped men and women alike in their tracks wherever she went—a beauty, combined with James's solid good looks, she was always careful to point out, that had been passed on to Beth and Maud in stunningly different but equally fabulous ways.

"You could be right," she found herself saying as they stood close together on the back porch. "Just promise me one thing?" She turned her face to catch his eye and he looked at her, sideways and just a bit down and smiled ruefully, knowing that when he looked into that face he would promise her anything. "You'll talk to the girls, too, before you make any plans for next summer?"

James screwed his head a bit more in her direction and his eyes gleamed playfully. "Okay! This year we'll be very democratic about it. No more King James," he only half joked. He let his body swivel slowly to face her and they embraced warmly, slowly, drawing each other closer as the sun's spectrum played over the sand. It always ended like this—no matter what the word game, the charade, or the puzzle that their daily life set in delicate interplay to challenge the vulnerability of their two joined but very different egos—and Alison knew that it always would.

* * *

"I thought those girls would never go to sleep," James complained, folding his arms behind his head on the pillow.

"It's not very late—only eleven." Alison leaned over him to check the clock and he intercepted her, enjoying the soft thud she made on his chest.

"I don't care what time it is." He stroked her hair. "I just don't feel like being a parent tonight."

"Oh? And what do you feel like—"

"Take this off . . ." James fumbled with the straps on her gown.

The pale blue strip of gauze that was her nightgown fluttered to the floor. He rolled closer and felt for her in the dark room.

"Ahhh. That's better . . ."

Outside on the beach a crew slowed their tractor to avoid an errant volleyball. A man slid down off the lumbering machine, made his way to the fork-pronged plow front, and kicked the ball under the porch of the house. He climbed back onto the rust-colored truck and it bumped slowly down the beach, catching driftwood, shells, and stray newspaper in its claw.

"Mmmpphhhh," Alison mumbled.

"It's nothing, hon, just the beach crew. Go back to sleep."

A body's length from the house a prone figure raised itself and turned to watch the receding tractor. Alden got to his knees, checked his camera for sand, and began to walk back to the rooming house.

Sunday was cloudy and the air felt like wet Kleenex clinging to steamed skin. While Beth did the ritual calisthenics on the soggy beach, Maud bemoaned the lack of sun with only one day of vacation left. Convinced that she would show up at school in a week's time as pale as a sheet, she settled for a thick layer of moisturizer which, her mother promised, would save her leathery hide until school began.

Because of the unsavory weather, they started early, packing the boxes and suitcases that seemed to increase in number every summer, though James and Alison had vowed this year, as every year before, to cut back on luggage and paraphernalia. An oversized carton marked "garbage" stood in the middle of the living room and gradually reached overflowing as the contents of kitchen cabinets, magazine racks, storage bins, and "junk drawers" made their way to the trash. Convinced that cleaning was terrific exercise, Beth pumped a vacuum with her right arm while attempting a few pliés with her legs. Starting with her exercise obsession, the conversation quickly shifted to the upcoming softball season.

"It's real important for me to have strong arms and legs this year since they moved me to left field," Beth shouted over the roar of the vacuum.

"Why did they move you?"

"Oh, you know Mr. Baker. He thinks I'm getting too tall for the infield. Moved me up in the batting lineup too. I bat sixth now, instead of eighth."

"Smart move," Maud piped in with a mouthful of milk chocolate candy. "Then when you strike out there'll be two more after you to save the game."

Fighting the urge to sweep her little sister away with the dust, Beth turned toward Alison and James, who struggled to hide the smiles Maud's comeback had brought.

"You guys really should do something about all that candy she eats," Beth settled for in retaliation. "It's starting to rot her brain."

"Tact and discretion," James mumbled under his breath to Alison. "Tact and discretion—the new catchwords for modern parenting."

"A lot you know, anyway, dummy," Beth continued. "Moving me up's a promotion! Your big sister's gonna be a star this year. Just wait and see!"

The threat of another day like Sunday passed overnight and Labor Day was hot and clear with crowds descending on the beach before the Sommers had finished breakfast. Though no concessions or public rest rooms besmirched that section of beach, day crowds had found the mile-long trek from the nearest parking lot well worth it to bask in clean, relatively uncluttered sand. Compared with the big public beaches Oceanview was like paradise.

Instead of the traditional barbecue party to close the summer season, neighbors on this stretch of beach had decided on a community volleyball game, picnic, and fireworks for the last-day celebration. Coolers of beer and sandwiches appeared in the shady spots underneath porches and scores of children clamored for the chance to play in the game.

At last, evenly divided among adults and youngsters, the big game began with extras rotating in as they were needed. Beth, all muscles and self-confidence, scored most of her team's points and went off for a cooling swim after her rotation as Alison replaced her in the back row. Tied after more than an hour of play, James stepped in to save his team's game and accepted the challenge to play two-out-of-three.

A blistering two hours later, having met the dare and won game three, James led his sweat-soaked team into the ocean for a long, relaxing dip. Food followed in abundance as the usual home phone numbers were exchanged along with pledges of midyear get-togethers and promises to keep in touch. Friends swore they would return next summer and pick up "right where we left off" as mothers, knowing the truth about most summer friendships, nodded to each other in a secret exchange.

The sun was uncooperative about setting and fireworks didn't begin until nearly ten—too late for most of the families who had long drives ahead of them the next morning but not too late for them to give in to the cajoling whines and "pleases" of their kids. Gradually, one by one, the families said their goodbyes and wound their way up and down the beach, disappearing at intervals into the houses that rimmed its border.

James crawled around in the sand under the porch picking up paper plates, napkins, and plastic cups and tossing them to Alison. Maud had long since fallen asleep on the sand and James stopped his cleaning to carry her to bed. Given a reprieve from cleanup, Beth followed her sister and Alison and James took a moment to embrace in the moonlight on their last night at the beach before resuming garbage detail. While Alison sat cross-legged on the beach, James dragged a large garbage bag to the side of the house and tied its ends securely.

A bright glint on the sand caught Alison's eye and she inched over to the spot, feeling about for a piece of stray glass or surf-polished shell. Her hand met a round, smooth-faced object and she held it up to the moonlight for inspection. It was something she had seen thousands of times in her life as a model but which was strangely out of place there on that suburban stretch of beach. Black, about two and a half inches in diameter and a half-inch thick, it felt a bit strange in her hand in that place and time. She looked at it again for a few moments, trying to decide whether it was worth saving, whether she should bother mentioning it to James. Then, with a shrug, she tossed the lens cover away.

As planned, James woke the girls early and the tiresome process of loading the car began. Final checks under beds and inside drawers took place as Alison locked the windows and doors. Most of the other houses on the strip would be occupied within a week by their owners but, strangely, this one always remained empty throughout the year. Still, Alison

33

liked to leave it neat and tidy and made one final round
tightening faucets and pulling electric plugs. Last to go
was the telephone, and as the phone man accepted his
tip and offered wishes for a "nice year" James ushered
the family toward the car. A row of bulging garbage
pails topped with overstuffed plastic trash bags and the
one, huge cardboard box of junk signaled their departure for the season.

"Damn!" James said.

"What?"

"I wish people wouldn't let their dogs run loose.
Just look at that!" The carton of refuse had been
crudely torn open along with two of the bags, and
newspapers, bottles, and a few odds and ends were
strewn on the curb and spilled into the street. James
left his car door ajar and went to clean up the mess.
The weekend papers, last week's magazines, some
soda and beer cans, fruit parings, and bits of junk from
various cabinets in the house kept him busy for a
couple of minutes.

"There." A slice of paper caught his eye, the back
cover of a magazine brought from home, the address
label now carelessly torn away. Rolled into a ball, it
too went into the damaged carton and James returned
to the car, brushing his hands against his jeans. Like
the missing address label on the errant magazine
cover, James failed, too, to note the sharp slice in the
cardboard carton. A slice that was repeated meticulously on both disarrayed garbage bags. A slice made
with a knife.

One by one, other families piled into other station
wagons and bumped down driveways to the street.
One of the few year-round residents, a young, attractive divorcee named Kay with two small children,
waved to Alison as she got into the car.

"Call me," she shouted across the street.

Alison waved yes as James began to back the car out
to the street.

* * *

34

The small of his back narrowed into the crook in the boardwalk railing, Alden faced the house while, with his camera, he focused on the dark, green wagon as it rolled down the driveway, edged into the street, and drove away. This time, external and very real, the sound of a click.

Chapter 3

PLEASE! Can't we? Please . . . Just for a little while? The Sommers car slowed at the highway exit marked "Amusement Park—2 miles." Alison stole a glance at James, subtly indicating her willingness to comply with Maud's plaintive request but wanting James to be the one to decide. The car sped up and passed the exit.

"Dad!"

"James?"

"I'm sorry. I forgot to tell you. I promised Arthur I'd stop in this afternoon to help get things started for the new semester."

"Oh, Jay . . . not again. Every year it's the same thing. Arthur Blackmore wants the week at home relaxing with his family so of course he calls upon you to go into that hot, stuffy building, before they've even turned the air conditioning on and do all the work alone. I thought we decided this year would be different."

"I know I promised it would be but Arthur called and told me Claire's sick . . . flu or something . . . and he'd like to spend a few days at home with her." He put a restraining hand on Alison's knee, feeling an outburst rising to the surface as she tensed in the seat next to him. Though part of him enjoyed her fierce protectiveness of his honor, he resented what went

36

with it—the implied criticism of having capitulated to his boss. "Look, I've been away eight weeks. Let me give the guy a break, will you?"

It was clearly the wrong response and Alison was defensive instantly. "And how much of those eight weeks have you spent *off* the phone? You know, James, it's hardly been a vacation for you."

"It's been a terrific vacation—hasn't it, kids?" He checked the rearview mirror for signs of support but was greeted by two sulking faces on scrunched bodies in the back seat. "Spoilsports!" he said playfully. "Come on, you guys, why do you think I became a college professor in the first place? It's because they always give you the summer off!" He grinned with forced energy but failed to elicit the desired response from wife or daughters.

"You know, that is sort of funny when you think of it," Alison went on, "because I don't think you've really had a summer off since you became Arthur's assistant."

"Associate," James was quick to correct her.

"Whatever. The point's still the same. And don't tell me all that nonsense about how Arthur Blackmore discovered you toiling away at that private high school and immediately recognized wasted talent when he saw it because I just don't buy it. Arthur Blackmore was just looking for someone he could mold into his own image so that when he had to retire there would be a Blackmore clone waiting in the wings to carry on in the big man's footsteps." Even Alison was surprised at the degree of resentment and anger in her tone. As far as she was concerned, Blackmore was the only thing standing in the way of James becoming head of the fine arts department and James was too blinded by what she saw as misguided loyalty to see it and make his move.

"I think you're forgetting one very important thing here, that Arthur thought well enough of my ability as a teacher to get the university to pay for my Ph.D."

"So, why spoil a perfect record? I paid for your first degree." Alison was sorry the minute the words fell from her mouth and drew her slender body in even tighter, hunching into the corner next to the car door as if hoping she might slide through the crack and disappear. She hated arguing with James and now she had really cut deep.

"Beth! Close that goddamned window! No wonder I'm sweltering up here even with the air conditioning on!" James put a rapid end to the budding argument as Beth gingerly reached over and rolled up her window.

Damn him, Alison thought, now aching for a good fight, he does that all the time! Just when she is certain an explosion is coming and they will really get to air their thoughts and disagreements openly, and even though she dreads the idea of a real fight with James, he turns around and slams the door on her emotions, and refuses even to face the topic that started the problem in the first place. She turned back to look at him, half opening her mouth to resume some kind of dialogue but the look of stony determination on his face silenced her before she began. She closed her eyes and leaned back in her seat. A half hour later the car turned off the highway at their exit and headed home, its occupants still stewing in steamy, silent peevishness.

"Okay. Look." James broke the thick silence, as always, claiming the patriarchal right to determine when to abort a fight and when to announce that peace and goodwill were, quite arbitrarily, restored. "This is no way to end a vacation. I'm sorry." It was intended more as a cue than an expression of genuine regret since, of course, he had not precipitated the fight— instead seeing himself as the victim of Alison's superior wit, logic, spirit, and money. But he wasn't about to let his moment of staged control pass now. "That wasn't intended to be a soliloquy, guys. Now let's get on with it."

"I'm sorry too, Jay. I got carried away. I never

should have said what I did." Alison leaned over and planted a kiss on his cheek. She was genuinely sorry for what she had said and was equally furious at herself for letting that old weapon re-emerge.

"We'll go to the park next summer, okay, Dad? I'll be big enough to ride the roller coaster," Maud piped in.

"Ahhhh . . . but will I?" James laughed as Maud joined in with giggles. "Well, I'm a brave guy, wha'd'ya say we try it next weekend, Ms. Coppertone?" And the tension dissolved.

"I knew I should've driven back last week to turn the water on." James commented a few minutes later as the wagon turned into the driveway lined on both sides with brownish-yellow grass. "I miss one week and look at it! That's what I get for being lazy."

"As if you're *ever* lazy." Alison opened the car door just as the vehicle stopped an inch from the garage door. "Shall we unload through the garage or from here?"

"Let's do it from here. Then we'll have everything in the front hall for even distribution instead of stuck in the kitchen."

"Good idea. Oh, Maud . . ." The little girl had almost succeeded in sneaking across the street to visit a friend when her mother's voice summoned her back. "Unpack first, visit later!" came the command as Maud sulked her way back across the street to the overstuffed station wagon.

"You girls get started. I'm going to get the mail from Jim. Be right back," James called, and dashed across the lawn, through the man-made arch in the hedge and over to his neighbor's porch.

"Mom, it's so *hot* inside. Yeech!"

"Well, why don't you go and open all the windows and let some air in, Beth, huh? And take some of this stuff in with you!"

"Look at all this junk, will you?" James was back,

39

loaded with ten days' mail. "I think we got more this last week than the whole summer."

"Aren't you glad you decided to drive back every week and pick it up instead of asking Jim to send it? We'd still be waiting for last week's mail."

"Yeah. At least my weekly travels kept us in touch . . . they didn't do much else good." James waved his hand in disgust over the scorched lawn.

"It isn't that bad. It's already September. Besides, it's been a very hot summer. Everyone's lawn looks a bit brown. Let me see that stuff." Alison reached for the mail.

"No, no, no. This is much too heavy for your delicate arms. Grab a couple of those suitcases and I'll meet you inside!" And James bounded toward the kitchen as Alison followed.

"I don't understand it," James said a couple of hours later over coffee as the girls busied themselves putting their clothes and possessions away and adjusting to the cramped quarters of their bedroom.

"Look at this. Bills. Just bills. And junk mail. How could there be so many bills when we haven't been here for two months?"

"Hey, look at this, Jay." Alison held up a colorful, three-by-five-inch rectangle.

"What is it?"

"It's a postcard, but look at the front."

"Who's it from?" James took the card.

"Hey, that's us!"

"Strange, huh? That looks like this weekend, doesn't it? The volleyball game? Remember when it was all over you and the kids and I sort of congregated by the net and congratulated ourselves? And Beth punched the ball way up in the air? Well, that's it. That's when this must've been taken."

"Whose idea was this anyway? There's no message or anything."

"I don't know. One of the neighbors, I guess."

"Peculiar, isn't it?"

"Well, I think it's kinda nice. Different. You know, this reminds me, after the party that night, when we were cleaning up? I found something under the porch at the house. It was a lens cover, the kind they use on expensive cameras. I couldn't figure out what it was doing there so I just threw it away. But now I think it must've belonged to one of the neighbors. I should've held on to it."

"They're easy enough to replace. But that does explain it. One of our friends is probably having a good laugh over a bunch of pictures of us with mustard dripping all over our clothes and sand in our potato salad. Just how I always wanted to be remembered." He held up the postcard for another look.

"What's that?" Beth bounced into the kitchen upside down, her hands performing a function usually allotted to other extremities.

"I always knew this family was upside down and backward but this is taking it much too literally!" James joked and held out the postcard.

Flipping right side up, Beth took it and examined it closely. "Ugh. Fat!"

"I knew we could count on Beth for an enlightened comment." Alison smiled. "Have you anything else to add?"

"Who took it?"

"We were hoping you could tell us that."

"Don't look at me. You had all the crazy friends— I'm very selective. Besides, you know they'd have to drag me in front of a camera before I'd let anyone take my picture. It adds fifteen pounds, you know!" She looked knowingly at her ex-model mother as if sharing some very top-secret data.

"I have heard that once or twice . . ." Alison shook her head with a smile.

"Here, let me put it on the mantel." Beth grabbed the postcard off the kitchen table. "It's neat!"

"Well, what isn't neat is all these bills. I'm going to

battle the checkbook for an hour or so before going to see Arthur. Can you manage the rest of the unpacking without me for a few hours, Al?'' and James, accepting her resigned smile as a yes, gathered the mail into a pile and headed for his den.

Alison put the empty cups in the sink and began to unpack the summer dishes and put them away. An idea struck her midway and she went into the living room, stood and looked at the small postcard on the ledge over the fireplace for a minute, and took it down to have a closer look. "Just as I thought," she mused to herself. There was nothing on the back but a very neatly printed address and a single stamp. The card was postmarked Oceanview.

"Dinner."

"Coming, hon. Come on, girls, dinner's ready."

"In a minute, I'll be right there."

"Well, *I'm* starved!"

"My biggest fan." Alison took a hunk of bread from Maud's hand. "Could you manage to wait for your father and your sister?"

"I'm starving!"

"Isn't she always. Look at this, I grew this summer, I knew it." Beth displayed her softball uniform, which had, most distinctly, grown shorter. Her knees were barely covered by the pants and there was a definite gap between their end and her socks' beginning. The sleeves, too, had inched toward her shoulders.

"Mom?"

"I'll take you to Harvey's tomorrow and we'll get a new one, okay? We can't have our star outfielder showing up in an outgrown uniform, can we?"

"Thanks. And I'm not a star yet. It's my first year at this position."

"You'll be a star. You always are. Best third baseman to best outfielder. It's a cinch." Maud was unusually complimentary. Beth reached over and put a hand on her sister's forehead.

"Funny. She's not running a fever."

"Boy. When I yell at her I'm picked on and when I'm nice I'm picked on. Can't a kid get a break?"

"Sure, Maud. Thanks. I appreciate your confidence in me. I'll win the first game for you."

"You're welcome . . . Beth?"

"Huh?"

"Can I have the old uniform?"

"Ah-ha! I knew it! Ulterior motive revealed!"

"Why do you want your sister's uniform? Since when are you interested in sports, prima donna?" James had used this particular form of endearment for Maud ever since she was an infant and had shown a very selective spirit about which of Alison's breasts she would deign to nurse from.

"Just because."

"Yeah, why *do* you want it? You can still have it, just tell me."

"For Halloween."

"Halloween! My uniform? No way!"

"You just said I could have it. Didn't she, Mom, you heard her! No fair!"

"Maud. Beth. Enough. Now let's discuss this later, girls, okay? This is not the time or the place to be discussing Halloween costumes—no less fighting over them. I mean, it is two months away! In the meantime, Beth, why don't you just let Maud have the uniform." One look from Alison silenced Beth's rising outburst. "Who knows, maybe it will inspire her to do more exercise than merely lifting a fork to her mouth!"

A born referee, Alison had learned a little bit about raising two distinctly opposite daughters from living her early years with parents who rarely, if ever, agreed on anything. Mainly, when in doubt, punt. It wasn't that different at all, being in the middle of two constantly bickering adults and sharing a house with two

independent and vocal little girls. Both situations required balance, tact, common sense, and a large por-
tion of luck. Fortunately for Beth and Maud, if not for
Alison herself, she was better equipped at age thirty-
five to jump into the fray than she had been at age
eleven. Besides, the truck-driver appetite of ten-year-
old Maud had always been a point of humor around the
dinner table, given the fact that her tiny frame showed
no hint of where it all went. The phone interrupted the
bantering and Beth jumped to answer it.

"For you . . ." She held the receiver out to Maud.

"That's Lisa. Can I go across for a little while? Just
a while?"

"Half an hour. That's all. You'll see Lisa tomorrow."

"Hi, Lise?" Maud grabbed the phone. "I'll be right
over."

The rhythm of home life was quickly reestablished
and by noon the next day Alison felt the two months of
sandy, sun-filled vacation slipping behind her. Supermarket lines, one teller at the bank for twenty customers, and an un-air-conditioned army-navy store
were just the first of the "welcome home" signs. After
nearly two hours spent trying to get Beth perfectly
outfitted for the year's softball opening a week hence,
it was Maud's turn as she suddenly decided that she
needed new shoes for school. Then it was the supply
counter at the paper store—notebooks, pencil cases,
sharpeners, crayons, loose-leaf paper, and books,
book covers, paste—the works. At least school was
only a weekend away.

James, too, got back into the swing of things rather
quickly, confronting several dozen files stacked on his
office desk along with the requisite preschool-season
crises of all shape and magnitude that seemed to find
their way to his office door every semester. Arthur
Blackmore, the chairman of the fine arts department
and the man James considered to be his mentor, had

taken time the previous afternoon to fill James in on several situations that would have to be handled that last week prior to the beginning of classes. It would be left to James to counsel the students wavering on the brink of a major, to deal with the incompletes and transfers, and to handle the multiplicity of excuses that always accompanied the empty-handed student who had sworn to show up the week before class with a long-overdue term paper in tow. As much as all of this busy work seemed to annoy Alison, James actually found it quite pleasant. He liked the university atmosphere, stayed clear of the politics as much as he could, and took great pleasure in the mild tugs-of-war with students over a change of grade or a deadline on a class project.

Today, James welcomed the quiet, studious atmosphere in the dark, wood-paneled offices he shared with Arthur. No lines of eager students awaited his arrival and the pile of file folders was not nearly as ominous as when he first saw them the day before. He let his trim, tanned body sink slowly into the deep leather chair behind his desk and leaned back comfortably, hands behind his head, enjoying the dark elegance and comfort of the room before beginning to work. He let his eyes take in the breadth of the room— the chintz couch and antique coffee table where Arthur entertained faculty guests, the walls overstocked with art books and texts and references, the small, well-secreted bar that Arthur felt every sophisticated office should have, the old but valuable stereo, the collection of family photographs.

James got up from his chair and walked over to one of the bookcases where several pictures of his family mingled with a few of James and other faculty members, carefully posed at university events. He reached out to touch the gilt edge of a photo of Alison and the girls and let his memory drift back to a time way back in high school when he had wanted more than anything to be a professional photographer. He had, in fact, gone so far as to apprentice himself to a local genius in the high-fashion field during his first year of college in order to supplement a small scholarship and more easily get through his four years. He had quickly worked his way up from go-fer to invaluable assistant and his confidence in his own amateur work had grown enough for him to have submitted a few of his news photos to the school paper—some of which were published. But then, halfway through his second semester, a critical—and pivotal—event occurred in his life. He met Alison.

It was Alison Ames, then. *"The* Alison Ames," his boss emphasized as he introduced them. She was the top fashion model in the U.S. at the time, having won the coveted Model of the Year Award, not to mention covers on magazines from *Seventeen* to *Glamour.* In James's eyes, she was absolutely the most beautiful woman he had ever seen.

They were to work on a week-long shoot together, compiling stills for a large fashion catalog as well as a spread for a national women's magazine and James had managed to get friends to cover his classes for him so he could devote his full attention to the job. It was, as his boss told him, the opportunity of a lifetime. And, in a way, he was right.

Alison was unexpectedly accessible on the shoot, failing to hide away in her trailer like most of the other models James had worked with, and he lunched with her the first two days, working up the nerve to invite her to dinner on the third. She accepted. From there, everything seemed to flow with an ease that let them both know that they were falling in love.

But a peculiar thing began to happen to James at the exact time when the overwhelming passion of first love was overtaking him—instead of being motivated by the budding relationship between would-be high-fashion photographer and the nation's high-fashion sweetheart, he was oddly intimidated by it and it was shortly after that week that he changed his major from photography to fine arts.

Looking back after all these years, even with the wisdom of time and the logic of distance to cushion him, James still felt a twinge of something between remorse and bitterness as he recalled that sense of intimidation in Alison's presence. He felt that no matter how successful he became or how adept with a camera, he could never ever do her justice. Even now, fifteen years and two wonderful children later, that feeling was still with him—muffled and dulled by his love for his family and for Alison and by that rational and logical part of his brain that told him that it was his problem and his alone.

Then, there was the money. More money than he had ever dreamed one person—one woman—could earn in a year. Even years later, with James firmly established at the university as a tenured associate professor, with their comfortable house all but paid for, two cars, and enough left over for the summer home, James still felt a pang when the quarterly statements came from Alison's various investments.

And then, of course, there were his girls. His two daughters were growing more beautiful every day. Beth was sure to enter one day soon into some high-powered career unless (James was sure not to rule this possibility out) she gave in to the lure of a long stint as an amateur gymnast. Even a scholarship to college was possible. But James was confident that whatever she decided to do, she would make it work for her. Both girls had inherited not only good looks but their mother's confidence and determination and James's verbal skills and intellect. He credited himself with having kept his insecurities hidden from them and, so he thought, for the most part from Alison as well. He was a good father—that he was certain of.

Quite the opposite of Beth was Maud, always the delicate one. James had always figured her to be an actress or a model like her mother—her temperamental nature and fine-boned features aside, she just seemed naturally to be the one to follow in Alison's footsteps. On family outings it was always quickly brought to attention by friendly observers, who never failed to notice the striking family, that Maud was a carbon copy of her mother while the lanky, athletic Beth inherited her beauty from her handsome father. In fact, James noted, holding a family photograph a few inches' distance from him and letting it catch a ray of sunlight that shot onto the brass-edged surface and refracted off the ivory-and-gold-tone telephone console on the desk nearby, those casual observers weren't too far from wrong.

There was Beth, clad in last summer's gym shorts and matching tanktop, her shoulder-length dark blond hair tied in a ponytail behind her and stuck through the opening at the back of a red baseball cap. Standing, as she was in the photograph, in front and slightly to the left of her father, the resemblance was uncanny. The straight, perfect nose, slim, strong face, brown-green eyes, and tall, slim but well-toned body paralleled her father's features exactly and, though only twelve at the time, she had the look of a much older girl—well trained and disciplined in the art of maintaining a healthy body.

A smile passed over James's face as he slid his eyes an inch to the right and focused on the duo of Alison and Maud—twins if he ever saw them, give or take twenty-three years—noting the dark, softly curling hair that framed their faces, the huge doe eyes, darker in tone than the hair, and the soft, sensuously pouting mouths. No doubt about it, those two were born to break hearts and, at least in his case, to win some. When it came right down to it, James thought as he put the photograph back in its place on the shelf, he was a very lucky man and he would see to it that there were nothing but good things in the future for him and his family.

With that thought the telephone interrupted his solitude. He watched a second light blink on the phone panel as he took the first call. Life at the university was back to normal.

Alison stood in the front hall and leaned against the wall as she talked softly into the telephone. From her position near the entrance to the living room she could see the mantel above the fireplace upon which there now sat three glossy colored postcards.

"I don't understand it, James. They came in the mail today. Two of them."

"The same thing?"

"No. Well, yes, I mean, they're us again—pictures from that last weekend at the beach."

"Don't let it upset you, Al. You know what it is? It's probably Kay, that's what I think. It has to be Kay."

"But why would she do that? I mean, the first one was kind of cute, but three? It's bizarre."

"Why don't you just call and ask her? You know Kay, she always was a bit strange; she probably thinks it's all a big joke to keep you from forgetting your promise to call her."

"I suppose you're right. It's the most sensible explanation. Maybe I will call her. I just can't understand why—"

"Allie. Do me a favor? Don't build this all up into something, okay? Just call her—no maybe's—just call and ask her what she's up to. Period."

"Okay. Okay. I'll call. I'm sorry to upset you at the office. I'll see you later, okay?"

"I love you."

"Me too. Bye."

Alison put the phone into its cradle and stood at the edge of the living room, eyeing the postcards. James's tone had been reassuring and his manner confident. Maybe it wasn't so wrong for him to have gone back to work a few days early. She liked him this way. And he

49

was right, it wouldn't be such a bad idea to phone Kay and ask her, just for the hell of it, Alison thought. She picked the phone up and dialed before the inspiration left her. No answer.

Heading for the kitchen, Alison wiped stray dust from the molding on the wall and decided a good house cleaning would take her mind off the mysterious cards. Besides, she smiled as she thought of Beth, she could use the exercise.

A comfortable, middle-class home in a neat, suburban community, the house had been just perfect for them and the very young Beth, and James had been so proud at having been able to afford the down payment that even if she hadn't loved it she would never have let him know. It was a disappointment giving up her career so young but as soon as James graduated from college and got his first teaching job he had brought up their "deal"—she had supported him until this job, now he would support her. As Alison recalled, her mother had been even more upset than she was— devastated, "mortally wounded" were her exact words, Alison smiled—she thought Alison should keep working as long as the camera was kind to her and earn as much money as possible "for a rainy day" but Alison held on to her conviction that those days only come if you ask for them. By continuing to work and earn more than four times what James did, she thought, she would be inviting trouble with open arms. Despite their problems, theirs was a stable marriage and, after all, that was the choice she had made. Besides, she tried to lighten her mood as she hoisted the vacuum from its berth in the storage closet beneath the stairs and flexed a slim arm, she still had the figure she showed off at age eighteen—not bad after two children. She shut the door on the storage closet, attached the vacuum, and began to glide it in long strokes across the floor.

The house was laid out very simply with a straight

staircase dividing it evenly in two and forming a sharp right angle at the top landing. From the front hallway, tastefully done in black and white linoleum and decorated only with a brass telephone table and coordinated phone, one could head directly for the thickly carpeted staircase and disappear upstairs in a flash. Crossing the hall perpendicularly, a similarly patterned linoleum strip led to the left into a matching-carpeted living room with a small, working fireplace. To the right of the hall, a square, white-walled room with a huge bay window served as a small dining room and opened into a bright, gaily wallpapered kitchen. A small bathroom and attached garage completed the first floor and, as Alison vacuumed the last corner of the kitchen and swung the hose over her shoulder to head upstairs, the sound of rock-and-roll music greeted her from the girls' room.

Upstairs, a master bedroom topped the living room and, with private bath and enough space for two soft chairs and a color TV, provided a pleasant sanctuary for Alison and James's infrequent, as of late, quiet times. To the right of the stairs, a second bedroom outfitted with two twin beds and enough stereo equipment and records to open a small store was home to Beth and Maud who shared the third, and largest, bathroom. James's den completed the house unless one was to count the dusty crawl space above the bedrooms that served as storage space.

For some time the Sommers had planned to expand the house upward, adding a third bedroom where that crawl space was and thereby allowing the girls their much-clamored-for privacy. The three years spent vacationing at the Oceanview summer house only intensified the need for another bedroom, and as James categorically refused to relinquish custody of his den and the adjustment of moving from separate rooms back into a single one year after year at summer's end grew more painful, Alison knew the time was rapidly approaching when that storage space would have to be converted. Hopefully, she thought to herself without much real hope, Arthur would finally retire and relinquish the reins to James's capable hands. Then, according to James, there would be enough money to begin on the expansion of the house. But until that time—and Arthur Blackmore showed no signs of being tempted by early retirement—the girls would have to continue to coexist. She wouldn't even broach the subject of paying for the new room herself. That, she laughed despite the seriousness of the problem, would literally raise the roof! About two years ago a naive Beth had dared to suggest that Mommy had enough money to pay for a new room, so why did they have to wait for Daddy to get his promotion—that could be forever. It took nearly two weeks for the air to fully clear back then, and now, with James beginning to really feel his oats at the university and, subsequently, at home, Alison was not about to cause trouble.

The sudden blare of heavy-metal rock music followed by a piercing shriek from Beth only confirmed Alison's feeling that there would be trouble one way or another. A third bedroom was the only solution, with luck, sooner rather than later.

"Turn it down. I said, turn it down. . . . Damn it, Maud, you're the most selfish, horrible pig I ever knew."

Alison interrupted Beth just as she was warming up and pointed a warning finger, stopping her eldest daughter in midscream. Maud opened her mouth to add a comment and was also silenced by the same finger.

"Maud, turn it down!" came the decree. "And Beth"—the smile disappeared from Beth's face—"if I ever hear you scream like that again, I'll see to it that you don't get out of the house for a full week—softball or no softball. Am I clear? Good. I'll call you for dinner, girls." Alison went back to her vacuuming, closing the door on muffled rock and roll and two glowering faces, lip synching curses at each other.

The sound of loud, tinny music insinuated itself into Alden Smith's small room and the sudden piercing shriek of a child's voice jolted him from a pleasant, foggy daydream. He lay, stunned by the sound, on his back in the middle of the bed and, when it did not stop, raised his hands stiffly to cover his ears. Tortured still by the bitter, mewling noise, he curled into a fetal position and buried his head in his chest. The music wafted over the child's teary cries and stabbed through to his consciousness, pricking away at him and leaving open, bloody sores that spread and sponged up the terrible noise. When he could stand the sound no longer, he rolled off the bed and staggered to the open window, slamming it shut with force and drawing the drapes to further insulate himself from the noises that rose from outside. Still that awful, horrible noise jabbed away—brash, jazzy beat; a small voice plaintively whimpering in high-pitched, grating tones; music growing louder and the voice suddenly raised to a screech, the sudden bloodcurdling squeal of a phonograph needle being drawn across a record and intense, tortured crying as the music whined to a stop.

Alden stumbled to the bureau, hands still over his ears, and thumped his forehead hard on the wood surface. A dazed moment later he looked up and slowly watched a reddish welt swell on his brow. He looked into the mirror in a stupor and tilted his head a small amount to the side, trying to catch a glimpse of an image there. It was Alden, just eight years old, cowering, runny-nosed, and streaked with tears in front of his hysterical mother as she tore the disc from the phonograph and smashed it on the floor.

The awful sounds inside his head faded and Alden dragged his feet on the rug as he went toward the bathroom and turned on the cold water in the sink, pressing his sore head under the faucet and letting the coolness soothe the nasty bump.

Unaware of the water dripping from his face, rolling down his neck and into his shirt, Alden walked back to the bed and lay down once more on his back, the faded floral print spreading evenly on either side of his bone-thin body and drops of moisture blending into the thirsty flowers on the worn cotton beneath him. He closed his eyes for a moment, more to set his focus than to rest and, when the desired memory had been brought up from storage, snapped them open again, and stared, unblinking, at the ceiling. There, in front of him, as clear in retrospect as it had been thirty-two years earlier was his boyhood room, and he, bopping playfully up and down to the tinny sound of music emanating from his cheap phonograph. He heard the heavy, angry footsteps then, watched the door fly open and his screaming, red-faced, Medusa-haired mother lunge toward him. Her mouth opened, all pink tongue and painted lips, and she spit curses at him while in his memory that simple, marvelous melody he used to listen to played on. Then, rising over the memory, the sound of his own voice, crying softly at first, then, suddenly aware of her intention, begging, pleading, cajoling, and finally shrieking and sobbing in fury as she lumbered over to the phonograph, reached out a flame-tipped hand, and dragged the needle cruelly across his adored record. Then, her pause, a gloating look of pure delight at the sniveling, shrinking eight-year-old before lifting the shiny black disc and smashing it on the floor. A crash—louder now in his mind than any sound could possibly be in reality—and it was all over. His mother slunk backward out of the room, her eyes lapping up last tastes of his despair as they flitted from the smashed record to the little boy's eyes. The door closed and he, on his knees, caressed the broken slices of his prize. Suddenly, without warning, there drifted over the scene before him the sound of that music again—jazzy, light beat, tingly tempo.

The crushed child faded, Alden blinked and the memory was gone. Left stupefied by its intensity, he pressed his head into the damp pillow and dozed.

Upon coming home from the office James went right to the fireplace and examined the two new postcards before going in to dinner. There was Maud, on the first one, bronzed and greasy on her beach chair with Beth in mid–jumping jack in the near distance.

The second card pictured the four of them, huddled snugly in blankets beneath the back porch, watching fireworks burst over the ocean. Again, as on the first card, the address was neatly, professionally lettered and a single, exactly placed stamp was the only other mark on both cards. They had been mailed from Oceanview.

James took them with him to the kitchen where he greeted Alison and his daughters and sat down at the table. As Alison brought a casserole from oven to table, James studied the cards. The quality of the photographs was impeccable. Balance, lighting, style—they had it all. Even to his out-of-practice eye it was clear they were taken by a professional. He had no idea Kay was such a good photographer.

"You know, Kay's pretty good with a camera. These are terrific," James said.

Alison put the hot dish on a trivet in the middle of the table, glanced at the two children, and went back to the counter to serve the rice.

"You did call her, didn't you, Al? I mean, these really are *good*. We should have her shoot a family portrait or something. Don't you think so, girls? Look how this one picks up the *exact* color of your tan, Maud. And Beth, it looks like you can fly. I'm impressed. These I'm going to save. . . . So, Alison, what did Kay say? Where did she learn to take such good pictures?"

Alison placed the plate of rice on the table and looked at James for a long moment, waiting for his bubbly enthusiasm to cool. He stuck a finger into the casserole and licked it off, smacked his lips, and looked up at his wife. What a serious look on her face. He sat back in his chair and waited for her to say something.

"I called Kay," Alison said, pausing again, too long.

"So? What did she say?" James had to prompt her. "Don't keep us in suspense."

"She didn't take those pictures. . . ."

Chapter 4

WELL, I hate it!"

"Maud, you just can't go to school in *that*."

"Why not?"

"Maud . . . your friends will see your tan . . . the whole world will see your tan. You just *can't* go to school in a beach dress and that's that."

"Okay. But I won't wear this either. I hate it."

"Well, then"—Alison guided the little girl to her overflowing closet—"find something we'll both like, put it on and get moving. It's almost eight!"

"She's not really gonna wear that to school, is she?" Beth had to get her two cents in. "I mean, come on, a diaper would cover more, for Crissakes."

"Beth!"

"Sorry."

"How's this?"

"Perfect." Alison gave a critical once-over to the short-sleeved, green terrycloth jumpsuit Maud held up in front of her. "Now put it on, you're late . . . and don't forget—no sandals. And do something with your hair." Alison's voice lingered in the room as the rest of her bolted downstairs to catch the overflowing coffee.

"Damn!" The brown fluid coated the gas range and dribbled into crevices beneath the burners. "Ow!" as she tried to mop up the mess with a flimsy paper towel.

"I always knew those paper-towel advertisements

on TV were right—if we just bought the right brand you wouldn't be in this fix." James sounded pretty cheery for this early in the morning as he reached for a terry towel to help mop up the spill.

"Just what I need on the first day of school—a walking TV commercial!" His cheeriness spread to Alison and she smiled at him. "God, I hate first days of school! *Girls,*" she shouted. "Move it!"

"Calm down. It isn't even eight-thirty."

"And they have to be there in fifteen minutes."

"They'll make it, it's just a few blocks. Here, let me clean that up and you sit for a while. You look really crazed." Alison gave him a look that said there was more on her mind than just getting the girls off to school—like what would come in the morning mail. "Forget about those cards, will you? I promise, it's nothing. Look, I'm gonna be late. I'll call you later, okay? Will you be home?" James stood poised to leave.

"Mostly. I just have a few errands, that's all."

"Okay." He planted a quick kiss on her cheek, dashed down the hall. *"Girls!* Let's go!" he bellowed up the stairs and let the front door slam behind him.

"I don't believe it. Quiet at last," Alison said out loud to the empty kitchen as she emptied the dishwasher and began to load the breakfast dishes. The coffee had left a crooked runway down the front of the white-enameled stove and trickled underneath its black steel border. Alison soaked a sponge in warm water before getting on her knees and wiping up the mess. As she checked for other coffee stains, a rustling sound outside distracted her and she glanced out the kitchen window in time to see the blue-clad figure of the mailman head for the next house. Feeling a knot form and twist in the pit of her stomach, Alison went to the front door, opened it, and reached into the mailbox.

Yes, there it was again. A postcard. She knew it

even before she actually saw the color photo. Gingerly she slid the card to the bottom of the pile and took her time sorting through the Monday magazines, bills, junk mail, and business letters for James until only the postcard remained. Like the others it was white-backed with the same small, neat postmarked stamp and the same dark, meticulous printing. A grayish-inked circle spelled out "Oceanview, Sept. 10"—just two days earlier.

Externally calm but with a heaving stomach, she flipped the card over and let out a startled gasp. The pile of mail slid from her fingers and scattered on the floor. There they were again, the whole family, only this time the photo touched much closer to home. In fact, it *was* home—the four of them, seated ever so comfortably in the brightly papered kitchen enjoying chicken salad, soft rolls, and Coke—last Friday's lunch. Panicked, Alison reached for the phone and dialed James's office.

"I'm sorry, Mrs. Sommers. He's not in the office right now. Can I have him call you?"

Alison let the phone slide back in its holder and reflexively knelt to gather up the mail from the floor. A fashion magazine had flipped open in the fall and as Alison was about to scoop it up with the rest of the mail she caught sight of a familiar face in a montage of photos on the glossy pages. It was her—more than twelve years ago in a photo, she recalled, that had received a lot of national attention—a seductive, highly revealing pose in a long, white, backless negligee. Somehow it had been dug up as part of this photographic history of lingerie modeling and planted in all-too-plain sight in this very popular and widely read magazine.

She brought it closer, studying the image, and lowered herself into a cross-legged position on the hall floor. Her eyes caught the caption beside it: "Alison Ames, at left, one of the world's most beautiful models, who gave it all up for the security of home and family." Suddenly, Alison found herself convulsed with uncontrollable laughter as all of the morning's tension exploded over her in a wave of spasmodic giggles. She clutched the magazine and roared for several minutes until tears came to her eyes and a painful catch in her side brought on a fit of gasping and coughing. She pulled herself up onto her knees, still clutching her side, gathered the rest of the mail which was now strewn over the hall floor, and got to her feet. She held the offensive postcard in her hands for a moment, wanting to tear it into tiny shreds, but fought off the impulse and placed it on top of the mail which she piled neatly on the hall telephone table. Then, reconsidering, she took the card with her to the kitchen where she stuck it in a recipe book and slammed the book shut. Determined to forget all about it until James came home, she went upstairs, took a long, hot shower, combed and dried her hair, dressed, and left to do her errands.

Conversation was light at dinner as Alison had made up her mind not to tell the girls about the latest postcard until she and James had figured out what to do. She focused attention, instead, on her discovery of the old photo of herself in the fashion magazine and, while noting James's discomfort at the topic, took delight in the pleasure it gave to Beth and Maud, especially since it made the need for any conversation about the postcards irrelevant at that moment. Later, when the girls were tackling their first night's home-work, she would show the postcard to James.

But she had not counted on his coming home laden with paperwork and the need to organize his thoughts for a faculty meeting the next morning. Nor had she planned on his falling asleep at his desk and having to be awakened at four A.M. to catch a few hours of sleep prone instead of pretzeled. By the time she arose to wake the kids, he had already left and any talk of the postcard was unavoidably delayed until that evening.

The postcards, though, didn't wait. A fifth one was there for Alison in the decorative, black-coated, stainless-steel mailbox outside the front door. At first she ignored it, gathering only the rest of the mail and trying to pretend that it wasn't there. But soon curiosity overpowered fear and she grabbed for the card, this time facing the image on its glossy side first before turning it over to see what she already knew would be there.

The picture startled her despite her preparedness and, upon seeing herself—freshly shampooed, attired in T-shirt and jeans with her new gingham scarf at her neck—pushing a cart full of food through the aisle at the supermarket—a scene she knew had just taken place the day before—she experienced a sweep of emotions from fear to terror to anger to fury to a terrifying sense of violation—what she imagined a rape victim might feel when being stalked by her attacker while never really knowing at what moment he would strike. Just who was this *person* to come barging in on her family and their private rituals and begin documenting them in such a bright, clear style as to belie the very underhandedness of the method? Just who was he to attack them with his private designs and infringe on their sense of themselves with his own, externally created impressions?

But with all her rage also came the painful, involuntary analysis of her own part in this, made tangible by the very existence of *her* image on the intrusive postcards. Perhaps what disturbed her most was the sense of rightness and belonging when seeing her face on those cards as if it was her rightful place, some kind of bizarre justice for having given up her true path in life and having sought to create instead some totally artificial reality based on a fairy tale of idyllic family life.

A stab of pain followed by a trickle of blood from a wicked paper cut caused by clutching the postcard so forcefully brought her back to the moment and with her calm, logical self back in control she waved away the thoughts of destiny and fate as schoolgirlish flights of fantasy. She had chosen her path of life, she told herself, with eyes wide open, heart unburdened, and mind clear and it had been the perfect choice. She sucked on her bloody finger and fought back the temptation, once again, to tear the card into shreds, instead moving toward the kitchen where she added it to the recipe book with the previous day's arrival and ran her bloody finger under a stream of cold water from the faucet.

"Ma . . . I'm home." Maud dumped her lunch box and sweater in the hall and raced upstairs to get a head start on her homework in order to be free in time for a favorite television program that began at seven. Alison emerged from the kitchen in time to catch a bit of her daughter's tailwind, but thought better of starting a scene over the discarded sweater and lunch box in the hall. In the mood Alison was in, it was better to avoid all fights if possible. Resignedly, she gathered up Maud's things, hung the sweater in the hall closet, and took the lunch box to the kitchen to wash it out for the next day. Alison flipped the metal clips on the box to open and set it in the kitchen sink just as the telephone rang. Lifting the princess receiver off the wall, she spoke for a few minutes, jotting down a brief message for James on the long blackboard that hung beneath the phone. Then she counted out potatoes to bake, selected the dinner dishes from the cabinet, and prepared to scrub the potatoes in the sink only to find Maud's rather grimy lunch box awaiting her. Alison lifted the sticky cover and turned the faucet on.

As the spray burst from the nozzle she pounced on the knob, shutting the stream off before it soaked the box, and stifled a rising scream of panic. Faceup inside the box, nestled in dirty napkins and crumpled tin foil, was a postcard of Maud, sitting cross-legged on her bed upstairs dressed in lacy white panties and pink T-shirt.

Alison choked back an urge to vomit in the box, swallowed her bile with her fear, and raced up to Maud's room, where she discovered her daughter, cross-legged and half dressed, scrunched against the pillows on her bed, tackling her math assignment. Reason having long since left her, Alison tore the book from Maud's hands and dragged the little girl off the bed, screaming at her to put clothes on and threatening dire occurrences if Maud ever again failed to draw the shades in her room before getting undressed. Having done nothing, until then, that was wrong, Maud simply cowered before her hysterical mother waiting for the siege to end and sanity to return. It didn't. Alison stalked about the room, pulling first shades, then drapes tightly shut, and tossing long-sleeved, long-legged clothing at Maud with orders to "cover up."

"But ma, it's *hot*." Maud's slight attempt at reason broke through Alison's rage and she suddenly saw the scared, confused child in front of her. Moisture forming in her eyes, she drew Maud to her and gave her an overwhelming hug.

"Oh, Maudie . . . I'm so sorry, baby. I didn't mean to yell at you like that. You can keep these on. Just *don't* touch the shades or go near the windows until you get dressed, okay?"

"Ma, you're squishing me." Maud wriggled free of Alison's embrace and started to pull on a pair of shorts and a top. Alison watched as Maud got dressed and selected her next words very carefully.

"Sweetie, did anything unusual happen at school today?"

"Uh-uh. Just the regular stuff."

"What about you? Did you have a good day?"

"Sure, I guess so. What's wrong?"

Alison made a note to remember that, these days, ten-year-olds have a lot more savvy than they did when she was growing up. She smiled at Maud and decided to take a more direct route.

"Nothing's wrong, Maud, I was just curious. For instance, I was wondering if you happened to notice anyone near your lunch box today."

"I don't think so. It was in my desk, mostly, till after lunch."

"What about later? Did you leave it anywhere?"

"Uh-uh . . . wait . . . yeah, I remember. Lisa and I were playing frisbee in the playground and I had all my stuff just lying on the floor and when I ran to catch the frisbee I kicked some of my stuff and my lunch box sort of landed over by the fence . . . you know, by the back of the playground."

"And you don't remember seeing anyone near it?"

"No. Why? Is it broken?"

"No, just dirty, that's all." Alison decided to cut her questioning short before Maud got curious or started to get frightened. "Try to be more careful with your things from now on, will you, Maud?" Alison said as she got up from the twin bed.

"Sure, Ma. Could I stay up an extra half hour tonight? Please?"

Alison grinned despite the concern she was feeling. "We'll see. Right now, finish your homework." And she closed the bedroom door behind her.

Downstairs, Alison went directly to the phone and dialed James's office. Interrupting him in the midst of another call, she demanded that he come home immediately, the tone of her voice offering the only explanation for her insistence. That tone frightened James as he had not heard it before and he felt the urgency in her voice grab at him. He cut his other call short, grabbed his jacket and briefcase, and raced for the parking lot.

He was home in less than half an hour, bolting through the front door and heading for the kitchen, certain that Alison would be awaiting him there. It was empty. He started for the stairs when a glimpse of movement in the hall mirror caught his eye and he saw

Alison, curled up on the rug in front of the couch in the living room, staring at a small mosaic in front of her. He walked to her side, held out his hand, and let her pull him down beside her.

"Six? When did these come? Why didn't you tell me?"

"Today. And one yesterday." Alison gestured to the shot of the family eating dinner. "They're all the same," she offered as James moved to turn them over.

"Oceanview?"

"All of them."

"Well, if someone thinks this is a joke, they're sure carrying it pretty far."

"It isn't a joke."

"Of course it is. What else could it be?"

"I don't know. But it's no joke." Alison's expression was too serious for James to challenge it. He watched her instead.

"Here. Look at this one." She brought James's attention to the postcard of Maud.

"My God. That's upstairs. That's *here.*"

"And these? Look at these . . ." Alison made James notice the locale of the other two cards. His lips tightened into a thin line and turned hard and white. Suddenly he knew it wasn't a joke.

"This is sick. These just came?"

"Well, sort of. I got this one yesterday." She indicated the first. "And this"—she held out the one of herself in the supermarket—"came this morning. But *this one*"—she was almost afraid to tell him, watched that tight, hard line that was his mouth—"this one"— she flipped it over, made him notice the blank, clean backing—"was hand delivered. At school. In Maud's lunch box." Her words came out clipped and hard. "I found it when I went to clean it out."

"Maud?" His first thought was for her, anger buried for the moment beneath concern and fear.

"No. She doesn't know. And Beth isn't home yet."

"We have to tell them. They have to know about this. This . . . this psycho could do something. He might talk to them, who knows . . ."

"I want to call the police."

"And tell them what? It's just postcards. They won't be able to do anything. Even if there were fingerprints, once, they're gone now." He indicated his and Alison's smudged fingerprints all over the cards and she let one fall onto the rug. "Look, I know how those guys operate; they'll come in here and scare Maud and Beth half to death with a police car in the driveway, and then they'll just tell us there's nothing they can do."

James went on, just a touch of frenzy entering his voice. "It's like an obscene caller—ignore him and he'll go away, let him know you're scared and he'll just keep on calling. Trust me . . . I can handle this guy." He reached over and stroked her hair, toned down the fear he was feeling in the face of hers. "If I really thought the police could do anything at all, I'd be the first to call them but this guy's gotta be just a crank. It'll pass. But just to be on the safe side let's talk to the girls tonight, okay? Calmly, no panic, but we have to tell them. They have a right to know what's going on."

Just hearing his voice reassured her and Alison let herself believe he was right. Surely this was just a freak incident—a crazy individual who had latched on to them in Oceanview for God only knows why and would get tired of the game as suddenly as he had started it. She swept the postcards into a pile, handed them to James, and started to get up from the floor as James reached for her, pulled her down, and embraced her strongly with a combination of passion and tension. She, too, felt the need to feel the physical strength of another body next to hers and welcomed his intense grasp and the rawly sensual kiss that accompanied it.

"You guys . . ." Alison and James looked up from

66

their cozy nest between the couch and the coffee table to find a mock-stern Beth standing over them clicking her tongue. They struggled to untwine themselves and get to their feet. "Don't you know there are minors in the house!" Beth giggled. James took a playful swipe at her bottom, just missing as she bolted out of the room and up the stairs, still laughing.

"Well, you wanted to have kids . . ." James teased, and embraced Alison once more as both their thoughts turned to more serious matters.

"That's right." James was telling the girls after the dinner meal had been cleared. "Three more cards. Two of them came in the mail and one, Maud"—he drew the girl's wandering attention—"was in your lunch box when you came home today."

"But I didn't . . ."

"I know you didn't, baby. But whoever this nut is he's watching us and taking photographs whenever he feels like it. Now he's probably harmless, but just in case I want you girls to be extra careful—here at home and especially outside. If he doesn't find anything to take pictures of, he'll go away. And if he knows that we know what he's up to and we don't show him we're scared, it'll take all the fun out of it for him and he'll stop. Now, I don't want you to change anything or stop doing what you always do—school, friends, softball. Just be aware, that's all. And if you're coming home late or you have to go anywhere alone, let me or your mother know and we'll drive you. It's just for a little while but that's the way I want it."

"Do you think he's here, right now?" Beth voiced the inevitable question, glancing toward the levelored kitchen window.

"I don't know. Maybe."

"James!" Alison watched the girls' faces go pale in fright.

"No. I'm not going to lie to them, Al. That's why we're talking about this. So they know. Yes, he probably is watching us now. Remember, he knows who we are, where we live. We don't even know what he looks like, it could even be someone we know."

"Oh, James. No."

"Well, it's possible. These things"—he indicated the postcards with disgust—"came from Oceanview. And we do live there two months out of every year. And how does he know where we live? Where Maud goes to school? Where you do your shopping? I still think he's harmless but we have to act like he's not. *We* have to watch out for ourselves. Now, listen to me, Beth, Maud." He waited for the two girls to look at him with attention. "There's no way I'm going to let this guy, or anyone else hurt you. You believe that, don't you?" They nodded yes, both serious and quite frightened despite his reassuring tone. "Good. Well then, you just do what I asked you to do and let me worry about the rest. You guys are the most important thing in the world to me and nothing's ever going to change that." He held out his arms and both girls got up from their seats at the table and went to hug him, long and hard. "Now, it's late and we've all had a rough day so why don't you two get ready for bed and I'll come up in a few minutes to say good night." He planted a kiss on each waiting forehead and watched his two daughters head for the staircase and disappear upstairs.

"How did I do?" He looked to Alison for a vote of confidence.

"You certainly convinced them."

"And you?" He already knew the answer.

"I want to believe you, Jay, I really do, but I'm so frightened. What if you're wrong and he really is dangerous?"

"I can protect my own family," James said sharply. "What do you want me to do? Buy a guard dog and hire a bodyguard? For Christ sakes, Alison, I thought you had a little more faith in me than that."

Alison stood at the crossroads of this impending

fight not knowing exactly what path to choose. Normally she would always opt for the most ego-soothing way to appease James but where the safety of her children was concerned his ego would have to stand in line.

"I always have faith in you, you know that. I just don't think either one of us knows what we're up against here and we should be prepared, that's all." She ventured close to him and put her hands on his shoulders, first meeting stiff resistance but then, as she began a gentle massage, sensing him relax under her touch.

"You're right. I'm sorry I blew up. I'm scared too. I guess we'll just have to wait and see. The next move is up to him." And he turned to catch a glimmer of fear that all-too-accurate assessment of the situation brought to her eyes.

It was growing dark outside and the room was shrinking in shadow, the fine lines and geometric definition Alden liked to focus on fading with the last rays of sunlight. On his back in the center of the bed Alden thought about rising to turn on the little yellow light under the mirror that hung above the bureau and played with the thought until the room was totally black. He finally groped his way to the opposite wall and turned the button on the base of the light to "on." A sick glow tinged the room and bathed Alden's already sallow skin in iodine. He went back to the bed, sat on its edge for a while, and then, almost hypnotically, slid back on the pillow, falling perfectly into the groove his body had formed in the soft mattress.

Alden had been in this room for more than two weeks and had not once opened the bed or slept beneath its covers, a habit that was held over from a childhood spent cowering in terror before a mother, herself a slattern, who, from his earliest days had forbidden—and viciously punished—the slightest variance from her decree that he maintain perfect, absolute invisibility. If he could not eat, drink, bathe, move about their tiny apartment, and take care of his own things without causing the slightest bit of disarray requiring her effort to clean up after him, then he would simply have to starve, dehydrate, stay dirty, sit still, and have no possessions whatever. It was clear from the start that he was a vile intrusion in her life. When he slobbered as an infant, she stuffed his mouth with paper towels. When he spilled milk as a toddler, he was forced to sleep in a puddle of it for three days on the kitchen floor. When he tossed and turned too much in his sleep and mussed his sheets and covers, she forbade him to ever again mess up the bed—even if it meant staying awake forever.

Thus, each night, now well into his fortieth year of life, he placed himself exactly in its center and, hands folded on his groin, eyes open and mouth still, he lay, corpselike, until sleep overcame him. When the chill of morning rattled his body, he would rise from the bed, watch the sun lift over the beach, and sip muddy coffee prepared in an electric hot pot the manager of the house had rented him for fifty cents a day. He didn't eat much either—a further remnant of his past, eating being such a difficult activity to monitor for error—usually a bag of potato chips, an odd piece of fruit, or a can of soup he purchased when out buying his film supplies.

On this particular night Alden wasn't hungry at all and he lay quite comfortably in his room watching the little yellow light with fascination. A stray thought prodded his memory and he stuck a hand out toward the nightstand, groping about for his target and then closing his fingers around it and drawing it to him.

Alden rested his hand on his stomach and looked at the small, brown vial with its white prescription label that he held in his palm. Carefully, he held it up to the dim light and studied it. He turned the bottle this way and that, catching flicks of the light on its surface and watching them drop onto the bedspread. Then, slowly and deliberately, he turned it upside down and shook it. Nothing. He shook it again. Still nothing. Alden stared at the bottle again for several minutes questioning its right to be empty. Then, condemning it for that choice, he suddenly closed it in his fist, crushing the hard, brown plastic with an uncanny burst of strength. Surging with that power, he sat up in the bed and tossed the vial away. Exhausted, he fell back, now sleepy, and wiped the incident from his consciousness.

Across the floor a smashed, twisted blob of plastic jogged into a corner and came to rest on its broken side, the edge of a white, sticky-backed label marked in clear, black type darkly stating: THORAZINE.

"Mommmyyyyy. Daddddyyyy . . ." Maud was sitting up in bed, clutching her blanket to her throat, sweating in terror at some unseen monster.

"Maud, what is it?" Beth jumped up to go to her sister but was rudely pushed away, tears now streaming down the younger girl's face as another jarring scream penetrated the dark house.

"Mommmmmmmmmmmmmmmyyyyyyy . . ."

Both Alison and James burst into the room, he flicking on the light switch and she rushing to Maud's bed.

"It was just a bad dream, Maud. Just a dream . . ." Alison cuddled her until the tears and shaking subsided. "Just a bad dream, that's all . . ." she repeated over and over to lull her daughter while looking solemnly over her shoulder at James's drawn and serious expression.

"Aaaaaaaarrrrrrghhhhhh!"

The scream woke Alden with a jolt and he lay, mesmerized by its power for a long time, only gradually realizing that it had come from deep within him, surging up to the surface with such speed that it had jarred him to consciousness yet left him dazed and confused. The dream that had given birth to that

71

terrifying scream was gone and Alden waited, sweating quietly in his grimy undershirt and jockey shorts, for an angry neighbor to pound on his door demanding quiet. No one came and Alden slowly knew that, again, his voice was floating in and out of reality—sometimes real, others imagined in the depths of his cruel subconscious. Like the little eight-year-old boy who, from nowhere, had emerged to torture Alden, this angry scream, too, had attacked without warning and Alden found himself unable to control the thought that these unwanted visitors from his depths would now come and go unmolested. He reached reflexively for his bottle of thorazine and, when his hand found nothing, remembered a few hours earlier discovering it empty. He lay back on the sweaty bedspread and stared at the ceiling as images from the dream that had jarred him awake played over the cracked, white surface and mesmerized him with their intensity.

Alden soon found himself hyperventilating as he came out of the painful reverie the dream had inspired and he tried to calm himself with long, slow breaths into cupped hands to regain carbon dioxide and then proceeded with a meditative loosening of his joints and muscles he had learned during all those childhood and adolescent years of having to remain motionless and unobtrusive in his mother's presence. Quietly, Alden began to count to himself. He counted the cracks in the ceiling, the flowers on the drapes, the lines and crevices on the dull brass frame around the mirror. Five, six, seven, eight . . . six, seven, eight . . . seven, eight . . . he fell asleep.

James sat on Beth's bed and surveyed the midnight scene through barely open eyes. As usual, Alison had been right. She had told him it would be a mistake to tell the girls about how that last postcard had arrived and had warned that it might bring just this kind of result.

"What was the dream, Maud?" he asked.

"I don't think it's a good idea for her to talk about it now, do you?" Alison voiced this as more of a rhetorical question than one demanding a reply.

"No. You're right." He was too sleepy to say the "as always" that was on the tip of his tongue. "Are you going to be okay now?" He turned to Maud. Her quivering body had become still as she dozed on Alison's shoulder.

"I'm tired." Beth unceremoniously made her desire for darkness and privacy known.

"Me too. Are you coming?" James walked toward the door and waited for Alison.

"I'll be there in a minute. You go ahead. I'm going to sit here for a while. Turn out the light." Alison gently laid Maud back down on the bed, adjusted the covers over her, and cuddled close, lying next to the small figure on the single bed and fell asleep.

Again it struck. That dreadful, awful swelling noise that pummeled his gut and turned him inside out. This time he wouldn't try to go back to sleep. This time it would win. It controlled him now, this crazed, insatiable, angry creature he nurtured unwillingly in his body. Tonight it would have its way. But soon, very soon, he would find a way to satiate it once and for all—soon he would restore the order.

Alden got up from the bed and felt the heat in the room surround and choke him. He went to the bathroom and, without turning on the light, reached behind the shower curtain to let the cold water run. Hot urine fizzed into the toilet bowl and he watched the last acid drops fall into the water, tucked himself back into the jockey shorts, and climbed into the shower.

He let his head ease back, the cool waterfall tickling his unkempt, brown hair, sliding over his face, Adam's apple, the jaundiced undershirt, and stale shorts. They clung to him in the coolness and he shivered, thoroughly enjoying the sensation of ice in his veins, the tiny goose bumps that appeared at the base of every

73

hair on his body. He let his slim, long-fingered hands rise and slid the palms over his face, smoothing his hair back and massaging his temples.

It felt sticky . . . suddenly sticky, hot, and carnal. He opened his eyes. The bathroom was still dark, a tiny stream of light filtering through the small window high in the shower wall. He looked at his hands, touched his face again, reached up to the shower nozzle. Sticky . . . hot . . . salty . . . dripping into his mouth . . . down his face . . . his pulse quickened, his pores tightened and he spasmodically drew a drenched hand over his mouth to quell the panic he felt rising into an inhuman scream.

"Blood . . ." he whispered to himself, fighting to get out of the shower. "It's blood . . . all over me . . . blood . . ." He slid on the slick surface of the tub, tangled his clammy, cotton-cloaked body in the plastic curtain, and stumbled from the tub. Dripping, he fumbled for the light, blinked furiously in its brazen suddenness, and forced himself to look into the mirror. No blood. He held up a drenched hand and traced his face and hairline with a finger, studied the finger. No blood. He ran both hands through his wet hair, squeezed moisture from his soggy underwear. No blood. Dazed and befuddled, he sank onto the toilet seat and buried his head in his knees.

An image came up at him from the tiled floor— smiling red lips, pink, soggy tongue. Sharp, yellowing teeth. That fine, shaggy mop of dark hair, bony cheeks, round chin. Suddenly it was Alden again, six years old this time, his hand on the knob of a door. It turned, opened. His mother on the toilet, her paisley skirt around her hips, white nylon panties down at her ankles. Her right hand slowly inched from between her legs clutching paper . . . white tissue . . . stained deep, bloody red. He was frightened. Wanted to run. Drawn by that gory stain . . . hypnotized. Then, she was up. Dragging her panties to her waist, grabbing him, stuffing him in the tub. A sudden flood of water—warm, red-dyed, sticky fluid. Bits of sopping, clotted paper, stench . . . it stopped. His mother stood over him, the wastebasket now emptied of its vile mix of urine, blood, and water drawn from the toilet. Disgusted, she turned on the faucet and left him.

It was cold in the room. Clammy. Shivery. The water was still running in the tub. The floor was soaked, the edges of the multicolored tiles blending into each other as Alden tried to bring them into focus. He pulled himself to his feet, his body wracked and broken by the vicious recollection. He looked carefully at himself in the glass, then removed the soggy underclothes and turned on the hot water in the shower. He stepped beneath the spray and, eyes open this time, let the heat penetrate his skin, nerve endings, blood vessels, muscles, tendons, bones. He was warm.

Alden got out of the shower and dried himself on one of the old towels that came with the room. He went, naked, to the dresser and fished for clean shorts, a short-sleeved white T-shirt. So dressed, he mopped up the bathroom with his towel, tossed it into the tub, and began to carefully mix and measure fluids in his developing pans. He unscrewed the lightbulb from its socket above the sink and juggled its hot surface in his hands, then replaced it with the deep, red bulb he used to illuminate his darkroom. When all was prepared he went to the bed and, leaning perpendicularly across its surface, reached underneath and pulled out one of his three cameras. Taking it with him, he closed the door to the john, flipped on the red light, sat on the hard toilet cover, and proceeded to remove a roll of exposed film.

The Sommers started the new day cautiously, none of them quite sure what to say or do about the events of the previous day and night. James had found Alison wrapped protectively around Maud in her bed and had

75

gently wakened them both to avoid jarring any memories of the night before. Beth, also, controlled her natural sarcasm and flippancy and even set about to make breakfast while bravely pretending that, as the older child, she was immune to the scaries of midnights. In turn, Maud, Alison, and James heaped praise on her cornflakes, instant coffee, and burnt toast. All trod gently that morning, and both kids jumped at James's offer to drive them to school.

Self-preservation coming to the fore, Alison made her decision to ignore the arrival of the mail as she watched James's light blue Chevy turn the corner toward the public school. Adamant about this decision, she went first to the telephone to enlist a neighbor, then to her bedroom to dig up her old tennis whites, and finally to the green station wagon which took her and Lisa's mother, Lynn, to the local tennis courts.

"Slam." A powerful stroke.

"Thunk." A good return.

"Slap." Darn. A miss.

"Boy, you're sure playing a rough game for someone who hasn't seen a court since last year."

"I know," Alison shouted. Then, "Thwack." A lob.

"Whew." A miss. "Let's get something to drink. I've had it."

Across the table in the coffee shop adjacent to the courts Alison described the strange occurrences of the past week to her friend and neighbor, Lynn Coley. A light-haired, easygoing type, Lynn listened with one ear, more to appease Alison than out of any real interest. Alison knew this, and felt that this characteristic was what had led her to choose Lynn as confidante. Alison had learned the hard way during her young, successful career years how damaging it could be to tell the wrong thing to the wrong person and, after many nasty brushes with the gossip-column press, the worst of which came directly after her marriage to James, she began to choose her friends quite selectively. She recognized it as a flaw in her character—this instantaneous distrust of anyone who showed too much interest or professed concern about personal matters—and had tried to avoid passing it on to her daughters while at the same time instilling in them a sense of caution like her own in choosing the inevitable string of "best friends." Here, in this situation with Lynn, she felt comfortable enough in the other woman's detached interest in her friends' lives to unburden herself without worry that gossip would spread. Not that Lynn wasn't a talker when she wanted to be, something Alison found quite endearing in the way it reminded her of her own adolescent friendships, but Lynn's talking always centered around things—clothes, the house, a new car, her hairdresser, their daughters' school, and so on. When it came to other people's problems, well, she just listened politely, paying homage to one of the duties of friendship, and forgot.

One lengthy and cathartic monologue later, Alison checked her watch as she sipped sugarless iced tea. A quarter to four. James had promised to come home early to pick Beth up after softball practice. She had better get going. She gave Lynn a peck on the cheek as they separated and could almost see her impassioned story of invasive terror fading from Lynn's memory, even as they left the coffee shop. By the time Lynn's husband showed up to take her to a friend's house for a barbecue, all but the pleasant and invigorating tennis game would have been forgotten.

James's car was already in the garage when Alison pulled in and she found him sitting in the living room nursing a beer and reading a journal.

"James?" She was almost afraid to ask.

"Huh?"

"Well . . ." His casual grunt piqued her curiosity. "Any . . . mail?"

"Not a thing."

The next day, too, the mailman brought the usual magazines, circulars, bills, and notices. There was even a small refund from the IRS. And not a single postcard.

"See," James told her. "I told you it was nothing. It's all over."

In his small, tidy room Alden sat at the wobbly, time-stained bridge table that served as his desk and a shard of sunlight cut across the surface. A neatly-laid-out quilt of prints formed a shiny covering there and Alden balanced his chair on its back two legs as he studied his work. Photograph after photograph gleamed at him. One, then a second, then a third he selected from the group, displeased with some minute imbalance in their composition. Deliberately he held the three over the wastebasket and lit a match to an edge, waited for the flame to spread, curl and blacken them all, then dropped them into the metal can to burn out.

Before him now, exaction—perfection was a word he had long ago learned never to use in relation to human subjects. A sheet of clear, precise, well-planned and executed work. He focused in on row after row. There were dozens of them. Pictures of Alison, James, Maud, and Beth at the beach house, on the sand, in the water, at home, and at work and play. Pictures of the children at school and of Alison in the supermarket. Pictures taken through the now-guarded windows of the house. And then, the final row, ignored by Alden as he studied his newest work. A family. Woman, two little girls. Closer. A woman strikingly similar to Alison in build and features, two young females—one a dark, curly-haired beauty; the elder taller, lankier, with straight, blond hair. And one, solitary, foreboding shot—an error kept as a reminder—never again repeated. A man lurking in lanky discomfort behind the brood—a part of them, yet somehow quite distant. Tall, lean, sharp-boned. Un-

78

kempt, fine-textured brown hair lazily brushed back from a smooth brow; a rebellious strand succumbing to gravity. And dull, staring brown eyes. Gathered with the woman and two young children into an awkward pose in front of a strikingly familiar two-story Oceanview beach house.

Alden Smith.

Chapter 5

WHEN Alden's mother robbed him of his wish to see her death at his own hand by having a fatal stroke at age forty, his long-festering loathing for her was left cruelly unconsummated. Instead, he was left with feelings of intense guilt over his matricidal fantasies which, in turn, led him to a peculiar juncture in his life. It was just a few days after her death that he noticed the ad in a local paper for "Grief Counseling," and while he knew that the blistering turmoil inside him was far from grief, he also sensed that it required venting before the heat of it burned him up inside.

And so he found himself amid a group of much older men and women, listening to the words of their stories without hearing the substance and magically awaiting the promised relief from his pain and suffering. Instead, he found himself courted by a young and quite beautiful woman, a social worker assisting the director of the group, who for some baffling reason took an immediate and intense liking for the shaggy young Alden that went far beyond what professionalism would dictate.

Despite four years of training and a hard-earned degree she was mysteriously drawn to this introverted, troubled, and subtly dangerous man and found herself pursuing him even as his intense and confusing feelings for her made him fight to withdraw.

When Alden Smith suddenly withdrew from the group after only five sessions and without so much as a word of explanation, she went after him, searching the local streets and shops for a sign of him and tracing any meager clues that might reveal his whereabouts. When her efforts succeeded, it was with much more than professional curiosity that she approached him, and as her passion slowly enveloped him, his uncertain resistance crumbled. For Alden Smith, the transition from camera to mirror was none too hard. Instead of seeing each frame of the world through a view finder as he had learned early on to protect himself, he began to see the world as a reflection of what Anise Spellman saw. If she felt happy, then it must be happiness that he felt. If she admired his strength, then it must be that he was strong. And if she felt herself in love, then it must be that he was in love.

Through her passion for him and her zest for life he experienced the edges of feelings previously alien and unexplored. Functioning, as she did, in an idealistically fantasized world that she alone could control, she emanated an excess of energy and emotion, a bottomless well for Alden to draw from. Providing a nurturing surrogate for all that Alden lacked, and with her stubborn, sure-minded aggressiveness, she guided them through an effortless courtship, quite without a master plan or even the conscious knowledge that she was doing so, planting the seed within Alden that this was the path he had chosen and that the light that refracted back from her was, indeed, a reflection of his own happiness.

When, at long last, he picked up on her cues to propose marriage, having avoided sex and thus precipitating some agitation on her part, she exultantly assented. It was a marriage quite without turbulence—even the common, everyday kind, and equally devoid of any but the most minimal physical or emotional contact. Conjugal obligations were grudgingly fulfilled, empty of passion, by the reluctant Alden, who nonetheless fathered a child not once, but twice. Thus, three years later, he found himself with a three-year-old girl and another female infant bawling in a crib and sought the comfort of view-finder eyes and F-stop vision as a wonderful haven from the intrusive noise and disarray of family life. Oddly, there existed too a peculiar sense of responsibility, almost of patriarchal fondness for these clearly imperfect but nonetheless his creations.

The three flitted around Alden's near-silent presence in the house like actors dancing around the aura of a dead playwright come to view the first performance of his final play. He was often there with them—accepting tiny morsels of food from a plate at mealtime, sitting unobtrusively in a corner of the back porch while they frolicked on the beach below, listening with polite distance to a poem or story read aloud by an enthusiastic child. And always, unused despite the pleas of his offspring, dangling around his neck from first light to last like some lifesaving prosthetic part of his anatomy, a 35mm. camera.

It was with abrupt and violent determination that the turnaround came when Alden learned of Anise's betrayal of a fifteen-year-old promise never to allow herself or their daughters to be photographed. The small modeling assignment she had accepted was without fanfare but when Alden accidentally came upon the photos, his response was swift and cruel, the weapon for her punishment the only one he knew—his camera.

It was the start of an unending stream of photos taken without pause or warning; expected and viciously candid, intrusive not only in their very sudden appearance in their lives but in the violent nature with which they took immediate and intractable control. Words of explanation were useless as Alden hid behind the protective mask of his camera at home, and stayed for long hours of private developing time after work.

Then, on the third sleepless night, he saw the answer. Carefully laying out a series of photos of his family, all classic examples of the cruel magnification of the imperfection of the human face that a camera was so adept at producing, he took a finely honed knife and began to delicately dissect each individual photo with the skill of a surgeon and the eye of a sculptor. First a separated eye, then a fine-boned cheek, the bridge of a nose, a singular smile, the turn of a child's delicate hand. One by one he unhinged the features from the whole, dissecting perfection into that which was innately imperfect.

Unlike nonhuman subjects, which, by the natural beauty of their specific angles and shadows allowed for no imperfection that the lens could not correct, their human counterparts were impossible to capture on film without every flaw being exaggerated to grotesque proportions. But here in his lab, by reducing the human face and body to a series of perfect angles and shadows, Alden had produced a miracle—he had found a way to correct the imperfect and restore order where there was inborn disarray. Gleefully, he went for the corresponding negatives and began to mark off matching segments and subsequently to print group after group of balanced, intricately detailed and incredibly perfect photos. Hour slipped into hour and it was nearly three A.M. when, bone weary but blessedly vindicated, he gathered the collection of finished photos, the good and the bad ones, and took them to the men's room where he had fashioned a hiding place behind one wall for his after-hours work. With the last of the photos secreted, he replaced the covering of the opening to the section of wall, carefully burned the night's negatives, prepared three bulk loads of film to attach to his three cameras, selected three tripods, meticulously packed his photo bag with all this, locked the photo booth behind him, and walked toward home.

Alden slipped through the back door and slid upstairs on silent feet, his photo bag feeling weightless on his back, despite the many pounds of equipment it held. Upstairs, he went first to his bedroom, took note of the softly sleeping Anise more for placement and centering than out of any sense of attachment, set up the first of the tripods at the foot of the bed, and placed a camera upon it with the prepacked, bulk load of film attached. In his elder daughter's room, he repeated the process and went on to do the same in the bedroom of his younger child.

The task completed, he edged his way back downstairs to the kitchen where his hand easily found the perfect tool that met the approval of his carefully measuring eye, and holding it close against his thigh, he returned to the staircase and glided silently back upstairs to the room where his wife slept.

A stray sliver of moonlight pierced through the nearly drawn blinds and shimmered over the edge of the symmetrically rectangular, white pillow. Conveniently centered on its down-filled surface, eyes gently closed, soft, curling brown hair forming a delicate frame, mouth open ever so slightly in the breath of sleep, Anise lay, faceup, beckoning him.

A raised, untrembling arm; a glint of steel grabbing the ray of moonlight; the poised elegance of a wood-handled meat cleaver. Balanced. Counting. The click, click, click of a shutter beginning.

Whack!

Alden closed the door of the photo shop behind him and let his sweat-soaked, blood-spattered body sink to the floor, hearing his mother's voice for the first time since her death, brutally informing him that he was a failure. He had made a mess of everything. And then, as quickly as the self-deprecation had started, it turned to his subjects—it was, after all, their fault. He had worked it out to the last minute and perfect detail. Damn them for having moved. Their defilement of his miracle—his all-enlightening discovery of the solution to the restoration of order; the ability at last to take perfect photos of human subjects—was one of unforgivable magnitude and he swore that they would pay.

A hint of impending sunrise warned him that he could not stay until he realized that it was Sunday and he had the entire day to himself. Slowly he got up from the floor and removed his spattered outer clothes. He went to the sink, turned the water on, and washed his hands and face, puzzled by the odd red color of the water that refreshed him. He checked his hands for signs of a cut that might explain the blood but, finding none, dismissed the thought as the water ran down the drain. More than eighteen grueling hours later he had processed the film from his three cameras, knowing full well the displeasure he would feel upon viewing the work but hoping that among all the photos, one or two would stand to vindicate him. None did. His task finished, he was now faced with 406 reminders of his failure to reproduce his miracle on film.

Each photo found its way to a place behind the men's room walls where some hundred-odd other photos had already been stored. Sensing some dampness in the wood, he searched for an appropriate covering to protect his work, but found insufficient paper in the shop to suit his needs. His eyes settled on his photo bag and he rummaged inside, came up with handfuls of neatly packed green bills, which he used to create a snug blanket between his photos and the mildewing walls.

His work finished, he replaced his outer clothes, took note of the approaching Monday dawn, recalled that he had ample film back at the house to repack his bulk film loaders, checked his cameras, and replaced them along with the three tripods in his camera bag. Giving the room a careful once-over to make certain there were no signs of his having been there, he closed the door behind him and headed for home and one more attempt at the failed miracle. In Alden's sadly distorted memory, all the events of the past night were merely the remnants of several failed photographs that could, quite simply, be set aright with a fresh batch of film and the determined resolve of a diligent artist.

He turned into the path that led to his house and his exhausted, adrenaline-drained body collapsed unresistingly under the weight of two burly police officers who pounced from the bushes. His arms drawn tightly and shackled behind him, his bag rudely thrown over a strange shoulder, he was led back down the familiar path and placed in the backseat of a police car. A few moments later, no siren disturbing the shocked silence of the street, the car drove away, leaving the house alone to bear the horrified scrutiny of curious passersby.

Chapter 6

A THIRD day without a postcard signaled an uneasy truce with the mails but apprehension trickled onto their daily paths, eroding the smooth mechanism of family life. With each succeeding uneventful day, new strife seemed to weave its way into the patterns of emotion and communication between James and Alison and brief but verbally violent arguments became frequent and easily triggered despite the fact that both of them knew that the cause of their short tempers was solely external. For James, the tension was represented by a nagging trickle of annoyance that the cards had stopped on their own without his having taken some definitive action and by a frustrating sense of self-doubt. Could he truly have protected his family had the cards turned out to be a precursor of some more violent action rather than simply the actions of a crank?

For Alison, the doubts and pressures were infinitely more complex, as she watched James's inner turmoil with growing concern. Watching the escalating frustration in her husband merely added to her own sense of inadequacy and embarrassment at being so readily available to this intrusive stranger and his all-seeing eye. That the cards had stopped coming was of little comfort to her as long as the sense of being watched remained and the feeling of being a prisoner in her own life continued to trap her. Knowing that when the cards resumed (and she had no doubt they would) James would be hard-pressed to control his anger or even to know what to do with it, Alison resigned herself to the knowledge that the physical protection of her family might, quite necessarily, fall upon her. With this knowledge also came a growing curiosity and near-obsession with their invisible assailant, her soon-to-be opponent. Secretly, late at night, she sat up and studied each detail of the postcards searching without success for some infinitesimal clue to his identity or, even more important, his personality. None presented itself.

Their two daughters had grown steadily more subdued in the wake of Maud's nightmare and the increasingly regular clashes between their parents. It was almost as if by ceasing, the cards had caused more damage than if they had continued, so tense was the household, so volatile the tempers of its inhabitants.

"We'd have been better off if they'd just kept on coming," Alison said bitterly. "At least then we'd be pulling together instead of tearing each other apart."

Perhaps, too, it was the uneasy return to routine that sparked the skirmishes, for it was not without backward glances that Alison frequented the neighborhood stores and James departed for the university in the morning. Maud had taken to carrying her lunch in a paper bag and kept vigilant watch on it until mealtime, after which she rolled the sack into a tight paper ball and tossed it away. Beth turned her energies toward the budding softball season with a vengeance and came home often too exhausted to eat—or to worry. Alison and James made love as frequently as they fought—and often with the same violent suddenness leading to an abrupt and often unrewarding purge. Neither the battles nor their lovemaking proved cathartic yet cyclical patterns formed in that brief period of days that left them sexually and temperamentally spent for a brief but enormously draining time to follow.

"Come on, Dana . . . *come on!* Hit one out. Let's go, Dana!" Beth bounced up and down on the hard bleacher bench.

"Whooooeeeeee!" as the ball landed far in the outfield. A triple.

"Of course *you'd* have caught that one for us, right, Beth?" her coach queried, only half teasing.

"Absolutely, Andy. For sure."

The Dreamboats had been number two in the junior female softball division for the past two years and this year they knew they'd make the move to first place. A few strategic changes in the lineup and the extra two inches Beth had added to her athletic frame almost guaranteed it. With Beth Sommers playing outfield, Coach Andy Parker hoped to be able to close that deadly hole through the left-field side that so many of the Dreamboats' opponents had successfully hit through the past two years. A crack shortstop in her younger days, Beth would make a terrific outfielder this year—she had the height, extension, thrust, and one hell of a throwing arm. Put her together with Dana DeLuca, the team slugger, and Andy knew he had a winner.

Today he had the 22 girls divided into opposing teams, each playing off the other's weaknesses so he could study their collective faults and make corrections in time for the season opener in ten days. Spectators were discouraged at practice games but Andy noticed with annoyance the few diehard parents clinging to the chain-link fence that edged the playing field. A man who firmly believed in strategic pressure on his players he nonetheless failed to support bench-jock parents who rode their kids so hard that a loss was akin to a major crime. Positive reinforcement, that was his method. No matter how a youngster screws up out there, find something good to say to her—pick on her strong points and she'll go out and bust her ass to please you. Tell her she's no good and you might as well fold the game. And it worked. Andy had seen these girls grow from flabby, disorganized children to toned, sharpened, dedicated amateurs. "Division title, here we come," he thought as number seven drove Dana home.

"Okay. B-team take the field," he shouted as inning eight came to an end. Beth's side was ahead 6–5 and she felt it her obligation to hold their lead even if it meant flying to catch a line drive. She jogged determinedly to her place on the left-field grass.

"Time." Beth flagged the bat girl to bring her sunglasses, signaled to the coach that she was ready.

"Play ball."

The count was three and two on the first batter when a short pop to right retired her.

Watching.

"Way to go!" Beth encouraged, waving a clenched fist at Dana who had made the putout at first base.

The second batter came to the plate, swung and missed the first curveball she faced.

A second pitch. Low and outside. The count went to one and one.

Moving in.
Closer.

"Crack." A foul tip. Upstairs, on the screen. The count now at one and two.

"Come on, come on," Beth said under her breath, wishing the ball to come sailing over her so she could spring up and grab it in her mitt. "Come on," she said as she danced from one foot to the other, prepared to leap in either direction to catch a flyball.

"Ball two."

"Arrrrrrggghhh." Beth growled.

"Wild pitch. Three and two."

Out on the mound the pitcher looked, set, and fired a fastball at the plate.

"Ball four." And the batter walked.

"One out and one on," Andy reminded. "Let's break this game open, girls. Put some life into it. That's the way. . . . Strike one."

The second stroke of the bat connected and a short drive up the middle was intercepted by the shortstop on a bounce. A quick toss to second and the runner was out on the force.

With two outs and one runner on base the next batter came to the plate, took a few warmup swings.

The first pitch . . . low and away. Ball one.

Arms extending—slowly.

A second pitch. Way outside. Ball two.

Another pitch. Fast ball. A swing . . . and a miss. Strike one.

The fourth pitch. High and tight. Ball three. Beth clenched her fist and pounded it into the glove. "Give me one right here," she chanted, "right here . . ."

"Smack!" The ball sailed right for her, arching and falling in a perfect curve above her glove.

Circling.
Arms high.

"I've got it . . . I've got it." Beth leaped as high as her long legs would push her, thinking "third out" all the way. Snapped her glove in the air at the flying ball. Landed. Her glove was empty. It couldn't be. Amazed, she looked at the ground and turned in a quick circle to see where she could have dropped the ball. Less than a foot behind her, a man. Tall and bony, gangly arms extending from a worn polo shirt. He stood over her a good six inches, stared blankly down at her stunned expression. He had the ball.

"Hey!" Beth stamped her foot on the grass, anger at his interruption of her perfect catch eradicating any trace of fear she might otherwise have felt at his sudden intrusion.

"Hey, mister . . ." He focused his eyes on hers, very slowly, then averted them slightly. Seemed not to know why she was speaking to him.

"The ball . . ."

He stared.

"Beth, what's going on out there?" Andy was heading toward the outfield.

Beth turned toward his voice, raised her hands in a broad shrug, turned back to indicate the interloper. The white ball lay on the grass evenly placed between two soft footprints. He was gone.

"How was practice?" Alison asked as she passed a plate of buttered carrots to Beth.

"We're gettin' there."

"Catch any fly balls today?" James knew Beth had been anxiously waiting for an opportunity to test her new position.

"Well, almost. It was really strange today. I was up for this ball and—"

"Ma, I don't feel well."

"What's wrong, Maud?"

"I feel sick. I think I'm gonna throw up."

"I'll take her. You finish your dinner," Alison said, and led Maud from the table and up to her room.

James and Beth continued eating silently for a minute, Beth hoping he would invite her to continue.

"I'm sorry, Beth, I'd better go up and see what's with your sister," and James was gone too.

The facade of privacy so tenuously yet hopefully erected over the past days was shattered with the arrival of another postcard on Saturday. This time it was James who discovered it and felt the initial thrust of its attack. It was very different from the others. Very, very different. He sat down on the front steps and looked at it closely. Queasiness slid over him like a shroud and he tightened into himself, palms sweating, muscles beginning to twitch sharply, overcome with a cancerous sense of inadequacy that clawed into his gut, gnawing at him, springing out of his own fears and insecurities and now flourishing quite independent of his weakening attempts to vanquish it and take control of his own destiny.

Daliesque in form and layout, the card eerily captured the natty texture of off-beige carpeting, stained bright red in a splotchy, erratic pattern that led haphazardly to a tiny, very white hand whose fingers clutched desperately at the carpet, pulling it in small ridges toward the infinite space beyond the border of the photo. It was a picture that cried out for more—for some explanation, some reason for this bit of disconnected, gory detail.

Clamping a vise of control on his wildly raging emotions, James got up from the stoop, went inside, and dialed the police.

It was just as he'd expected. Explanations, excuses, apologies, and platitudes. The officer who came to their door a half hour after James's call, McRae was his name, was nice enough, even compassionate toward the end of his hour with them, but helpful only in relative terms. Much of what he told them they already knew, in fact, had done after the first cards arrived. James's predictions as to the routinization of their complaint fell true as each of the pieces, dropped neatly onto Officer McRae's initially blank pad, slipped into designated spots in the policeman's prearranged mind.

Jotting notes as he spoke in a carefully trained, deliberately emotionless voice, McRae listed their ordeal under the topic of "random harassment" and thoroughly detailed in monotonous accuracy the "obscene phone call syndrome" which James had already compared to the postcard barrage. McRae made it clear that little, if anything, of substance could be done to locate the sender without some descriptive information to go on, however vague. It was also, he explained, rare for any sizable manpower to be assigned to a "nonthreatening" case such as this one, the implication being that until some direct physical assault took place on the family or their property, the police department couldn't do a thing.

The eventual explosive insistence of James that *something* be done, that the police department do its job, brought about the expected list of more important, "actual crimes" that needed immediate and thorough investigation, leading them to the inevitable and undoubtedly deliberately engineered conclusion that theirs was a paltry complaint indeed.

Glancing casually at the array of cards neatly set out for his benefit, McRae managed to stifle a slight twinge that, uncontrolled, would have turned into a full-blown shudder as the last card passed beneath his impartial gaze. Clearly, he thought, there was potential danger here, the progression of this jigsaw leading to what was (hopefully not) an inevitable climax in some crude and violent act. He inhaled softly, silently as his gaze wandered around the neat and beautifully furnished living room and settled on a small group of enamel-framed pictures of Alison in a variety of professional poses, her face and demeanor barely indicating that there was a period of several years between the time those photos were taken and the present. It was a favorite series of hers, and while James eschewed the feelings it brought about in him to see this lingering evidence of her successful, high-paying past, he did love to look at her. These were among the best pictures taken in the course of her career. Of course there were the requisite other photos in the suburban household, mostly family poses taken by James, or occasionally by a friend or neighbor so that James might participate in the picture as well. Officer McRae's eyes passed quickly over the several family photos with marked disinterest and glided back to the grouping of Alison's photos as an idea crossed his mind.

Could it be, he suggested casually to the Sommers, that in light of Alison's obvious affinity with the camera and the fact that she obviously had done some modeling in her time (he was genuinely astonished to learn that it had been fifteen years since her last professional appearance) this malevolent intruder was somehow connected to her past or, if not that, had come upon her quite accidentally in the course of the summer in Oceanview, recognized her face (he could be an old fan, the cop thought) and decided that he would personally correct his displeasure at her decision to abdicate the limelight for family life? In other words, some nut who had fallen in love with her pictures years ago, got mad because she quit, saw her one day on the street (she had, after all, changed so little) and decided to punish her for leaving him? A bit convoluted, he admitted, but possible.

"Anyway," he concluded, as he stood up from the couch, "it might be worth thinking about," and stooped to retrieve a photo and glanced surreptitiously at the image one last time before replacing it with the others. It was the picture of Maud.

"I'm sorry I can't be of more help right now," he said apologetically as the front door opened to let him out. James leaned on it, facing Alison, with what she knew was a look of blame and disgust, what he obviously believed was the absolute truth the officer had uttered. Here it was again, just one more example of the way her onetime fame insinuated itself into their life together, not enough to cause a collapse, but enough so that he could never forget, and she would always remember. Now, with the steady arrival of these postcards, there was further reason for James to

95

dredge up the past as if, in some way unknown to them both, she had secretly conspired with the sender to humiliate him.

"Hey . . ." Beth bounded into the house, unaware that her timely arrival had dissipated an impending argument. "What were the cops doin' here? What happened?"

"It's nothing to worry about, Beth," Alison answered slowly. "We just decided it was time to let the police know about the postcards."

"Why? Did we get another one?" And without waiting for an answer, "It's all over, right, Dad?"

"Yes, Beth. It's all over."

"I'm really beginning to love Sundays." Alison lazed on a lounge chair in the yard, enjoying the unusually hot and sunny September weather.

"Because I'm home?"

"Because there's no mail."

"It's Mondays I can't stand." Alison chewed on a nail as the mailman approached the house.

"Morning. Nice day, isn't it?"

"Sure is. Thank you." James took the bundle from the uniformed man's outstretched hand, sat on the top step, and thumbed through it.

"I knew it." He held up a colored card without looking at the image.

She cringed. "Oh, look at it . . . it's horrible!"

A wooden handle struck the eye at a forty-five-degree angle and the top part of a silvery blade glimmered, its edge buried deeply in soft flesh. A naked belly button. A river of blood. The image, as in the last card, disconnected. The style, as always, captivating. Riveting. The ultimate irony that, what these viewers saw as stunning artistry (quite separate from the revolting content) the artist himself viewed as his albatross.

Determinedly, James got up from the steps, marched into the house, collected the group of cards, and exited past a startled Alison. If the police couldn't do more than sugarcoat the situation or pass insinuations about his wife's past in lieu of offering protection, maybe the post office would.

"I'm sorry, sir. But you see, there's absolutely nothing we can do. We can't *screen* your mail for you."

"There is a law against sending this kind of stuff through the mail, you know."

"No, sir. I didn't know. In fact, the laws governing this sort of thing are very vague. Besides," the prissy clerk turned his nose up in disgust at the card James held before him, "I wouldn't quite know *how* to categorize that. It isn't quite obscene, really, and the style is awfully elegant. Sort of early S and M, wouldn't you say?"

James felt control slide away from him as he reached in through the narrow square opening rimmed in sliding glass panels and found the edges of the man's nattily tailored jacket. The explosion was abrupt and short-lived, the point quickly made. James released his grip on the man's clothing.

Shaking himself nervously, the clerk smoothed his shirt under the creased lapels and looked James icily in the eye. "I'm terribly sorry, *sir,* but I can't help you." And the heavy wooden slab that served as a notice to customers that a window was closed, fell.

"That's right," James spoke through the small crack in the manager's office door. "I'd like to see the manager."

"Have you spoken with one of our clerks, they're very helpful," the woman offered.

"Unfortunately they can't help me with this particular problem, ma'am. May I please see your superior?"

The door slid open. "You wanted to see me?"

"Yes, thank you." It was an answer dripping with relief. "My name is James Sommers. I'm having a problem with obscene mail that's been delivered to my house."

"Come in, Mr. Sommers." The man extended his hand. "I'm Mark Schaffer. Take a seat and I'll see what I can do to help."

"Unfortunately"—the expected response took only twenty minutes, this time, to be extracted as the man leaned forward in his chair after listening carefully to James's story and studying the postcards—"I'm afraid there's very little I can do to help. You see"—he raised an index finger for emphasis—"these cards don't fall into the category labeled 'obscene' and they aren't actually threatening. There's no message, no indication of who sent them or why they were sent; just this postmark, Oceanview, and that's out of our district. You might try tracing the cards through the local post office there, but it's my guess they've been mailed at random from local boxes. Frankly, unless you have an idea of who's sending them and why, I can't think of a darn way to trace them."

"Well, suppose I don't want to trace them, just put a stop to them. Can't you simply hold them and send the rest of the mail?"

"You're talking censorship there, Mr. Sommers. That's pretty serious. And illegal."

"Look, Mr. Schaffer, I'm not a fool. I'm a long-standing member of the community, a professor at the university. If I authorize you to remove any threatening or violent postcards from my mail that isn't censorship. In fact, it's your legal responsibility. As a taxpayer, I help pay your salary . . ." James's argument, as well as his stamina, was wearing thin. He knew the man was right. Holding the cards wouldn't stop them from coming, it would only stop him from seeing them—and thereby possibly getting an inkling of when something more dire might be ripe to occur. There really wasn't anything to do except wait.

"Come on, Mr. Sommers." The man labored the point. "You're an educated man, you tell me. Suppose I do take it upon myself to censor your mail—at your request. And suppose what I think is threatening or violent is totally different from what you think. Suppose I should decide to censor all your postcards and you just happen to get a card from your Great Aunt Rose in Boston that has a reproduction of that painting, *Veronica's Veil*—you know, the one of Christ in the crown of thorns with drops of blood popping out all over his head—and just suppose I decide that's too violent for your kids to see and I hold that one back. Well, you tell me, Mr. Sommers, just how quick would you be to get yourself some hotshot attorney and bring a lawsuit on me and this office?" The man's voice edged up just a bit as he controlled an urge to spout fountains of theory and opinion on the role of the U.S. Mail in obscenity cases.

"Yes, you're right, Mr. Schaffer," James conceded. "But tell me, is there anything at all I can do?"

"You've done everything you can for now. Take a post office box, cross your fingers, and hope it stops soon."

"Damn it, Alison . . ." It was another of the all-too-frequent outbursts that, this time, sent James's suddenly-empty chair flying backward onto the dining-room floor.

"James! Be careful, you almost broke it."

"Be careful, be careful," the tirade began. "Is the fucking chair all you can think of? Why don't you try remembering to pull the goddamned shades down?" James was livid as was usually the case when one of his safety precautions was forgotten. He pulled hard on the linen shades that blocked the view through the huge bay window and heard a loud "rrriiiippppp" as one tore from its roller.

"That's just great. Now what're we supposed to do? You could've just asked me to do it, you know."

"I did. I asked you yesterday, and the day before. I thought this was settled. When we're in this house the shades stay down. Period. Is that simple enough for you? What are you staring at?" He turned his anger suddenly on the two children who watched him with uncertain eyes at once intrigued and frightened by the rare outburst in their presence.

"Well . . ." It came a moment later, an effort at apology. "I'm sorry. I can't always be expected to stay calm and collected. I'm worried about you—about all of us. And I'm scared, too. Damn scared." He took the roll of masking tape Alison handed him and tried to repair the shade, not at all certain whether the burning fear he felt was at the unseen or at his own inability to combat it.

Diagonally across from the Sommers' front window, shielded from sight by the high edge of a railing that surrounded the roof of a four-story brick building that had recently been converted into a neighborhood arts and crafts center, Alden calculated with precision the exact placement of a tripod on the concrete rooftop. Finally satisfied, he carefully placed his camera in the exact spot and moved to set the focus. A slight adjustment of the telephoto lens, a minute alteration in the night sight, and his subjects came clearly into view. Angular in placement, the shot was nevertheless perfectly balanced and composed. Any variations caused by unexpected movement by the subjects could be easily cropped or air-brushed in editing. He was ready to shoot.

"Click. Click. Click." A series of shots snapped off. One of the subjects moved and Alden sat on his heels and waited.

Alison went to the kitchen and returned a few moments later with a huge white platter which she ceremoniously placed in the center of the dining-room table.

"Voilà!"

"I'm almost done," James called from his spot on the floor, "just give me a minute and I'll have it fixed. I'm sorry I blew up but I'm not sorry about insisting we keep the shades down. That guy could be anywhere . . ." He was sorry he said it. The two girls looked from him to their mother to each other. He decided to let the subject drop.

"You start. I'll be right there." He stood up and fit the ends of the shade roller into the little sockets at each side of the center window.

"Damn, damn, damn!" A slight tug on the shade had brought the whole canvas tumbling down again and the window was bare except for a few odd strands of masking tape.

"Just leave it until after dinner, will you? Everything's getting cold."

He hesitated, glanced cautiously out toward the empty street.

"Leave it . . ."

"Okay, okay." He came to the table. "Boy . . . does that look good!"

"Yeah, Ma. You should take a picture of that . . ."

Alden watched her settle into her place next to the girls at the round table and rose to his knees to check the framing of the shot. Balanced, just so, the three females were plainly in view—the male safely out of the frame. He looked closer. What met his eyes sent him reeling into the past and he careened back to that first bus ride on the day he'd left the hospital. That incredibly delicious, fresh, seaside smell, the ocean breeze, a plate brimming with steamed rice, a trim of ripe tomatoes, a red, red lobster nestled in soft whiteness. . . .

* * *

On the table, a lobster, freshly steamed and hot red, waiting to be cracked. A bed of white, fluffy rice. Round, ripe, red tomatoes.

"Click." His hand touched the shutter. An accident. "Click, click, click." This time inaudible but to him, internal, pricking at him, sending him back, further, further . . . He grabbed the camera, jammed his face to the view finder, tried desperately to stall the back-rushing past. Blackness. Swirling, boggy, thick blackness. Focus . . . I have to focus, he thought, turning the lens back and forth. Still nothing.

Then, racing toward him, a track of light, blinding, white. A hallway. A corner. Cowering child. A little girl, wide-eyed, mingled disbelief and terror. Pulverized trust. A glimmer . . . recognition? Then horror, defense, a small arm coming up to meet the honed blade. "Slice . . ." A rush of blood, screams, a soft thud. So much blood. Sloppy. The arm on the floor. Askew. Not as it should be. She lunging at him, barreling between his legs, knocking him backward. Crawling across the floor, down the steps. A trail of blood. Disorder. His dream—the miracle—to dissect and balance each image prior to framing it—shattered, splattered with blood. A tiny, blood-drained hand reaching helplessly, etching thin lines in the carpet. "Click."

Darkness. Cool air. The rooftop.

Alden shivered. He rubbed his eyes on his jacket sleeves and retuned the focus. How much time had passed, he wondered. They were done. A pile of naked shells and crumpled napkins in the view finder. A rush of music. Panic. Hands stuffed over ears. He crawled to the edge of the roof. Tormented by that sound. Louder. Magnified in his head. A cacophony of tones. Clanging, thumping, twanging. Where was it coming from? He raised his throbbing head just a little, looked into the street below. Lying on his stomach on the roof. Inflamed, tortured. He had to stop it. Handle it.

Calm it down. Control. "One, two, three, four, five, six, seven, eight, nine, ten, eleven, twelve . . . one, two, three, four, five, six, seven, eight, nine, ten, eleven, twelve . . ." he counted faster. Over and over again, each rooftop, every lawn, each single television antenna. He counted and counted them again, pressing the music further and further back with each litany until he couldn't hear it. "One, two, three, four, five—" He was interrupted. They were opening the front door. The music grew louder. A television set. Singing. He wriggled back to the camera, slid it down off its stand. "One, two, three, four . . . one, two . . . one, two, three, four, five . . ." he mumbled into his chest, folded the tripod together. "One, two, three, one, two, three, four, five, six . . . one, two, three . . ." He stuffed the equipment into his duffel bag, got to his feet. Slung the bag over his shoulder. Hands again pressed tightly over his ears. "One, two, three, four, five, six . . . one, two, three, four . . ." He made his way to the roof door. "One, two, three, four . . ." The door closed softly behind him.

There was a cool breeze and James wrapped his arms around Alison as they stood in the open front door and watched the dark, empty street.

"I'm really sorry about all that," he said.

"It's been rough on all of us."

"The girls . . ."

"It's all right. I don't think they heard everything. Besides, we're going to have to tell them about it sooner or later. As you said, he could be watching us at any time. Anyway, they don't really believe it's over because they know we don't believe it. They're pretty smart cookies, you know? You can only pretend everything's all right for so long."

James looked at her quietly. As usual, she was right.

"Do you think it will ever stop?"

"Of course it will. It'll run its course. It's just taking a little longer than we thought."

"But what if he . . . ?" She shivered and he drew her closer to him.

"He won't. I promise you, everything's going to be just fine," and James kissed her softly as they turned to go inside, wishing he had more faith in the power of promises.

The dead bolt clicked into place and the front light went out. A rustle in the hedge that separated the Sommers from their next-door neighbors. The crack of breaking twigs, torn leaves. A scraping, sliding sound. Dragging. A small thud. Footsteps.

Alden had crawled the length of the hedge to the street, his bag thumping behind him. A long scratch rose on his hand. A trickle of blood. He sucked it off. A car passed and he ducked, waited. Walked to the bus stop and felt for coins in his jacket pocket. A soft wind was blowing and he zipped his light tan canvas baseball jacket up to his neck. Headlights. The bus was coming. Quickly, Alden pulled his camera from his bag, stepped off the curb into the street. There. Not perfect but interesting. A strong angle. Caddy-corner now, the house half out of view—not the best shot. The streetlight brightened his hand. A trickle of blood from the middle finger to the thumb. He set the focus. A drop of blood on his right shoe. The bus was there.

"Click."

Chapter 7

IT was unusual for Alden to awaken so late. Already past ten, he felt that sluggish, weighty feeling that sleep left him with in any but the smallest doses. He raised his right hand to rub his eyes, stuck dry and tight with the excess of rest, and studied the deep, scabby zigzag that ran the three inches from his middle finger to thumb. Where had it come from? He remembered. The hedge. Last night. He traced the line gently with the index finger of his left hand. Caked blood made the cut appear wider and sloppier than it really was.

He inched slowly up to a sitting position, his legs straight out in front of him on the bed, and examined his injury more closely. There was a stain of blood on his shirt about midway between his waist and bottom rib where his hand habitually rested during sleep but the balance of the wide-spaced flower pattern on his bedspread had not been disrupted by any stray drops. He would have to fix the cut. Minimize it. Make sure it would heal cleanly, not leave a scar. The presence of this error on his flesh disturbed Alden, and the longer he looked at it the more he felt the need to eradicate it. He swung his stiff legs over the edge of the bed and, feeling the first flows of circulation return to his sleep-clogged limbs, stumbled clumsily off to the bathroom.

He studied the cut carefully for several minutes,

examining it first from his angle directly above the outstretched hand, then checking it from a distance as it reflected back to him in the bathroom mirror. As if airbrushing a photograph to perfect a minor flaw he eased the offending hand under the faucet, turned on cool water, and gently scraped the dried blood and red-black scab from the scratch. A tiny brook of fresh blood sprang from the wound and he let the trickle of water wash it into the sink. There. He could see the outline of the cut clearly. A finely spaced, angular scratch like a wide-spaced Z that shifted slightly when he flexed his hand. It would heal nicely now, possibly not form a scar. He turned the water off, wrapped a wad of toilet paper tightly around the cut, and held it securely in his fist.

Maneuvering awkwardly with his left hand, Alden took the electric hot pot from its place on the bureau and, returning to the bathroom, filled it with water. He plugged the cord first to the green metal pot, then to the wall outlet. In less than two minutes a red light flashed, alerting him to the imminent boiling of the water. He took his cup from beside the pot and opened the top drawer of the bureau where he kept the jar of instant coffee. He unscrewed the top, dipped a bent spoon deep inside. The clink of glass. The jar was empty. Angered, he raised his left hand high to smash the jar against the wall, felt the urge pass, and lowered the bottle to his side. Even without the numbing effect of the habitual thorazine he knew that unwarranted bursts of anger usually led to chaos, then much time spent rearranging the segments of his life again. In all, a waste of time. He fumbled in his slacks, twisting around to stick his uninjured left hand into his right pants pocket, and came up with a crumpled bunch of bills. Good. He twisted the bloody tissue paper off his hand, examined the cut for traces of still-fresh blood, and, satisfied that it had stopped flowing, put the bills back into his pocket and, pulling the plug on the water heater, left to replace the empty jar.

The supermarket was a few blocks' walk from the rooming house past the drugstore, newspaper stand, boutiques, toy shop, and the barber's. Still struggling beneath the weight of sleep he couldn't seem to shake off, Alden walked erratically, stumbling every now and then, stopping to lean on a lamp post or post box for momentary support, occasionally missing one of the well-spaced cracks in the sidewalk that he usually tried to land squarely upon with each deliberate step. He plodded forward, eyes down, until he found himself in front of the food store. Inside, a blast of cold air shocked him awake, and he slapped his arms around himself to keep warm. Confused by the maze of aisles loaded with row after row of brightly labeled boxes and cans of food, he oriented himself slowly, counting each aisle, each visible row of food, the lights that marked the ceiling into an even pattern, the checkout counters. Now calm, prepared, he ventured forth into the puzzle and searched the signs above each lane for the one that would say "coffee." There. He found it. Smiling ever so slightly, he made his way to the aisle and turned in. So many brands. Such a variety of shapes and sizes. He stared, transfixed by the choice. Reached out blindly and closed his hand around the nearest jar marked "instant." He should have brought the empty jar along with him for duplication. He felt the glass shape in his hand. A sudden noise—what was that? A child. Whining. Bitterly demanding its mother's attention. He winced. Louder. It was coming from behind him. He clutched the jar tighter, his hand still extended straight ahead, wrist resting on the edge of the shelf. He caught a glimpse of the cut on his hand, bleeding afresh now, a thin trickle dribbling down his hand toward his jacket cuff. He pulled it back toward him, shifted the coffee to the other hand. Turned swiftly. A wall of jars, boxes, and cans. That child still screaming.

Alden raised himself up to his full height and peered over the top of the row of boxes that ridged the aisle. A shopping cart, laden with food, a dirty-faced little boy trapped in its front cage, chubby legs dangling helplessly over the floor. A few feet further. A woman, her back to the child and to Alden, overweight thighs bulging out of plaid bermuda shorts. A pink T-shirt outlining fat blobs that rimmed her bra line. "Number forty-three." Alden shifted his vision upward toward the voice. A glass and steel counter. Bright yellow lights. A wooden slab, silver weight scales, a roll of shiny white paper. The heavy, rhythmic "chop, chop, chop" of a blade hitting the wood. He stood mesmerized.

Behind the counter a man; bald, gleaming pate, ruddy cheeks. A white apron drenched in carnage. Bloody hands. A pile of gore; the loud "crunch" of breaking bones. Splattered redness. A rush of warmth, surging pulse rate. Alden clutched the edges of the shelf before him with both hands. The coffee bottle slid to the floor. Hard, beveled glass rejected the surface and rolled instead of smashing. Came to rest in a crevice beneath the peanut butter jars. Alden traveling backward now, speeding, catapulted into that time again, his hand bleeding into his jacket sleeve, his memory bleeding into the past.

A kitchen. White, sharply lit. A speckled enamel counter. A chopping board. The "chip, chip, chip" of a cleaver severing meat from bone. Silver blade meeting pink flesh. Spellbinding flash. Chopping. A small, grimy hand outstretched. Reaching, reaching for that redness, the enticing slice of silver. A bloodcurdling scream. A flash of sharp pain. A sliver of child-flesh lying atop the ground meat. Human blood mingling with the night's dinner. His hand now held high, his weight supported on that single, aching socket. Alden's mother shaking him across the kitchen floor by that throbbing, stinging arm. A spray of blood flying everywhere she swung him, painting the white surface of the refrigerator, the hard, clean tabletop, the linoleum floor. Dropped. Suddenly seated heavily on the floor, the edge of his palm stuck in his mouth. Warm, salty taste. That cleaver poised now inches above his head. His mother ranting, waving the blade, enticing him closer. His palm stabbing him; raw, stringy flesh. A violent swing of the cleaver, dismissing him. A damp, smelly puddle on the floor where he had lost control, soiled his pants. A trail dripping behind him. His mother beside herself. Hurling threats. The cleaver furiously pounded into the bloody chopping board. A spray of meat and bits of bone obliterating the small slice of little-boy skin.

"Chop. Chop. Chop. Chop." The bald-headed man was going about his work, the woman eagerly observing, a pink tongue flicked briefly over painted lips. A deafening howl. The little boy kicking, tossing the wagon from side to side. The woman's hand rising, falling to "smack" on his face. A flood of tears. Dirty stripes on his cheeks. Blue-white snot rubbed on his arm.

Slowly Alden moved forward, drifting, easing him toward that carnage. Floating movement, effortless glide. Sliding toward that redness, the glint of steel. Easing, easing forward. Closer. A few more steps. Unstifled motion. A dreamlike pace. The meat cleaver. Symbol of his imperfection. Tool of its inevitable correction. Further existing in his memory— beyond that childhood scene—shrouded. Another time—his hand on the wooden support, the blade falling to other flesh. Beckoning. Passing the screaming child. Faraway, painless cries. The pudgy mother. The clean, bright glass counter.

Head cocked sideways, glazed eyes, trapped between then and now. A slow arc, sweeping movement. Sudden landing. The soft, slithery "squish" of warm, blood-soaked flesh between his fingers. Squeezing. Oozing redness. A furious yell. Shocked, tumbling back to the present. A crowd. Mumbles, whispering.

That man, coming toward him with a vengeance, swinging the bloody hatchet. A flash of his mother's face. A wall of people parting; gasps, the throng subsiding into emptiness. The man looking up at him, muscles bulging on meat-stained arms. The blade hovering. A sideways glance. His hand, buried in chopped, runny flesh. A chill. His hand extracting itself, drawing back. Alertness. Speed. A sudden pounding of his sneakered feet as they dashed down the aisle, past his forgotten coffee, jellies, jams, apple butters, olives, pickles, and canned soups. Crashing to the door. A stunned obstacle. Focusing. The word *in*. Backing quickly. A turn. Dashing again. The doors parting. Escape.

Behind him, running footsteps. Vile epithets hurled at his back. The short, strongly built butcher pursuing him, that sudden, piercing yell that had jarred him back—spitting from the man's lips. A bull-like arm swirling the bloody ax in the air. The bald head sweating. Red, angry cheeks. The swiftness of a taller, slimmer Alden. The added pace of fear. Sudden bodily recollection. The past remembered in a reflex. Sphincter released. A long, hot spurt of urine down his pants leg. Panic. Speed. Silence. A cautious turn. The butcher, heaving from the chase, bent over. His elbows on his knees. Catching his breath. The cleaver at his side. Over.

"Watch it or I'll cut you!" The barber pulled his pointy scissors back from Hamilton Arnold's hairy neck just as the man swiveled in his chair to catch the commotion outside.

"Never. You're too swift to miss a trick with those scissors, Nate."

"There's always a first time. Besides, there's nothin' to see."

"Sure sounded like somethin' to me."

"Yeah. Everything sounds like somethin' to you . . ."

110

Ham looked up at the man snipping away at his salt-and-pepper hair and narrowed his eyes to a slit.

"Now, don't give me that tough, salty-dog look. I know what you're about, Ham Arnold, and don't you forget it. When a man's been cuttin' a fella's hair for as many years as I been cuttin' yours, well, he gets to know 'im pretty well."

"Well, since you're such a smart devil, you know I'm itchin' to know what just went on outside. What'd you see while you were snippin' away back there?"

"Just old Duffy chasin' some wild-eyed guy out of the store. Probably tried to steal himself a good meal. Quite a sight, too, old Duff wavin' his knife like he was a pirate or somethin' about to slice that poor guy to hamburger."

"He catch 'im?"

"Naw. One thing about Duff, he ain't too quick on his feet!" The two men laughed at the image of the short, stockily-built, heavy-muscled butcher trying to outrun anyone.

"Yup," the barber went on, "town's full of them crazy guys just out o' that hospital outside o' town. Lousy shame they dump 'em all on us. Can't work. Laze around all day, pickin' garbage. Waitin' for their welfare checks. If you ask me, they should all be locked up, permanent. . . . There. All done."

"They've been releasing people from the state hospital?" Hamilton's curiosity was piqued.

"Surprised you don't know that. New policy says 'treat and release.' Ain't no money to keep those guys locked up forever, I guess. Been in the newspaper."

"I haven't seen it." Ham's voice was edged in bitter sarcasm.

"That'll be ten bucks . . . come back soon."

"Always do. . . . Got change for a twenty?"

"Sure. Fixed up the house any?"

"Some. You know how it is . . ."

"What you need's a woman's touch. Now if you an' Edna'd just tie the knot . . ."

"Now, you know me, Nate. 'Never mess up a good thing' is what I always say!" And with a hearty laugh he was at the door. "See ya in an inch or so. . . ." He smiled and was gone.

"So they've been releasing people from the hospital . . ." he repeated to himself as he headed across the street and toward a bench on the boardwalk. "Damned if I didn't even notice." He shook his head at the apathy that had surrounded him these past four years, a trace of the reluctance that had kept him from the memories of another, painful time.

Close to twenty years earlier, at the not-so-young age of forty-one, Hamilton Arnold's carefully plotted path had led him to the small, seaside community of Oceanview where he decided to put his years of experience as press liaison for the United States Army and, later on, as a freelance journalist, to good use by taking a job as a reporter on *The Crest,* Oceanview's reputable, albeit small, newspaper. Sam Duncan, the paper's hard-boiled publisher/editor had found Ham, plastered and belligerent in a rotting seaside bar a few miles out of the town one midnight and had offered him a job. Oh, it wasn't quite that easy, he recalled later, but it sure beat going the interview route. Actually, a drunken swing of Ham's fist had caught Sam's attention—and his chin—and he had pinned the drunken Ham to the floor in a display of strength unusual in a man in his late 50's with four rounds of whiskey in him. A sobering while later the two men had joined hands over a final stiff drink and Sam had placed his business card—and a copy of the paper—in Ham's bruised fist. Next day, nursing a powerful hangover and a bruised lip Hamilton Arnold applied for—and got—the job of reporter of local news for *The Crest.* It took Sam Duncan nearly two weeks before he learned of Ham's extensive background in journalism, his more than 20 years' experience in the field.

Ham had risen from associate editor to editor when, at sixty-seven, Sam Duncan suffered a stroke while putting the paper to bed late one night, and a slow recovery made it impossible for him to continue working. Hamilton took on the job with zeal, determined to keep things alive until his friend recovered.

At fifty-five, after fourteen years in Oceanview, Ham had become something of a legend in the town and he loved it. A gruff, grumbly mutt of a man he nevertheless managed to attract every stray dog and child in Oceanview and coveted the not-altogether-true image of himself as all bark and no bite.

Still lean and trim, he worked out every day on the beach, punishing his body with rigorous calisthenics, running, stretching, and playing basketball. Occasionally he would take on teams of local kids in a one-on-six game of impossible odds. Packing a mean right hand, he pummeled a punching bag in his driveway for thirty minutes each day and rode a bicycle the four miles to and from work with regularity. Standing five-ten, he felt taller and walked high, his strong chin jutting forward. Gray had spiced his hair at an early age and added feisty character to his craggy face with its piercing yet warm blue eyes. A hairy man, he wore his shirts open a notch at the collar and rolled his sleeves up above the elbows, letting unruly curls of gray-brown fuzz spill forth.

Women adored his teasing gruffness and he could be the life of the party, often was, when he wasn't chasing down a hot story. For most of his years in that town, though, his heart had belonged to Edna, the local librarian with whom he shared a comfortable, on-again-off-again relationship based on the foundation of a solid friendship. But marriage was never to be in his future and one of the strengths of their bond together hinged on her unquestioning acceptance of that unchangeable fact.

Hamilton Arnold had been married once—it seemed for only a brief moment—way, way back when the

113

cruel reality of war had made the search for love in the bombed-out ruins of London a healing necessity. His wife was a young nurse, barely twenty, whose own parents—like Ham's—had left her an orphan at a very early age. A four-day leave was the start and end of their courtship and they married before Ham went back to the war. She had become pregnant during those days together—as many of the women in the towns and cities of Europe had when life in a war zone seemed to grant them only so much time with their men, and Ham watched with bursting pride as she grew larger each time he returned on leave. A baby girl was born two weeks premature, and Ham missed the arrival, having scheduled a long leave for her due date. A popular and much-decorated young officer, he was able to wangle a two-week pass—the happiest fortnight of his life.

Three months later his wife was dead, killed in an air raid which destroyed their London flat. Miraculously, the child had survived and was in the care of friends. Back in London, looking on her tiny face nestled in soft yellow blankets, Ham knew he could never be a father to her. The legacy of an orphan was not to be for his daughter but a heartbroken war rogue such as Ham for both father and mother was no better.

Using well-earned connections, he arranged for a solid, private, and very secret adoption with a highly respected army captain and his lovely wife—unable themselves to have children but clearly blessed with the will and temperament to be good parents. With her picture close to his heart and one final long look, Ham left his baby girl in their hands and went back to war and the army career that, for the ten years it lasted, afforded him the time to heal and the chance to surreptitiously observe the growth of his only child, still bearing the name his wife had chosen for her and now carrying her adoptive surname—a name she would always believe to be her own—Anise Spellman.

After the war, when Hamilton was offered, and

accepted, the job of press liaison for the army, he found himself able to participate vicariously in his little girl's life without his true identity becoming known. A few years later, when Captain Spellman died, Ham was sorely tempted to let Anise know the truth but her adoptive mother convinced him not to destroy the girl's fond memories of the man she knew and loved as her father.

Contented with his own, successful life, he enjoyed the freedom bachelorhood brought while at the same time delighting in the private secret his past always kept close to him. Each time mother and daughter relocated to a new city or town, Hamilton Arnold, too, conveniently popped up just arm's distance away, enjoying the simple pleasure of an occasional glimpse of his growing daughter and the off-and-on bit of news her mother passed to him in rare phone conversations or chance meetings.

When Anise left home for college, Ham spoke at length with her mother, offering financial assistance and any other help that might be needed but found himself graciously turned down by the independent Laura Spellman, who had put away an ample nest egg for Anise's education. He graciously bid farewell to Laura Spellman and relocated to a comfortably small apartment close to the college that Anise was attending.

It was during the next year, when Laura Spellman unexpectedly died of a cancer they thought was cured, that Ham faced the roughest period in his distant parenthood. Quietly attending the small funeral and witnessing the inconsolable grief of Anise, Ham wanted to rush to her and hold her to his chest, telling her that she was not an orphan—that he, her real father, was and always had been there to protect her if she needed him, and always would continue to be.

As he glanced at the faded, worn baby picture he still carried in his wallet, he almost did tell her the truth but logic and the realization of what the truth—if

115

she would even believe him—might do to her already fragile spirit, warned him away. He settled instead for quietly introducing himself as an army friend of her father's and was pleased and surprised to learn that she had noticed him several times during her young life both at army functions and the infrequent meetings with her mother. Flattered, he offered assistance and companionship during the hard days that followed, seeing it as an opportunity to get to know her better and perhaps, at a later time, to tell her the truth about their relationship. But, quite like her adopted mother, she chose the steadfast route of independence and adulthood, settling her mother's affairs quickly and competently, leaving much in the hands of a good lawyer, and returning to college and her future.

Convinced that this young woman no longer needed a daily watchdog, Ham accepted the position of stringer on a renowned, national magazine and, from his small apartment base, traveled extensively, though never for too long, for the next four years. Always touching base long enough to quickly check on her progress and happiness, it was with great concern and apprehension that he observed her insistent pursuit of a disreputable-looking young man who appeared one day at the counseling center where she worked.

His fatherly antennae were immediately aroused. He began to investigate the man with a fervor usually reserved for his most passionately involving news assignments. In spite of a very sketchy past that told Hamilton almost nothing, it was an eerie message that came between the lines, that made the hairs on the back of his neck stand on end. Or perhaps it was just the sight of the gangly, unkempt, and dead-eyed man walking with his little girl that set Hamilton's radar on edge.

All Ham had been able to learn was that Alden Smith had no police record, no army service, no driver's license, and had never voted. He kept a small apartment, always paid his rent on time, in cash, and had graduated a few years earlier than Anise from a community college, with honors in photography and poor grades in all else. He worked as a photo developer, avoided trouble, had no family, and never made friends. On top of that, he didn't smoke, drink, or sleep around and the few people who ever bothered to notice him had nothing unkind to say. He was just a quiet, introverted odd kind of guy who kept to himself, rarely smiled or spoke, and blended into the woodwork. It all made Hamilton damn nervous.

When the relationship escalated into marriage and then into pregnancy, Hamilton followed the Smiths to their new home in Oceanview, where, if he couldn't change the path of his daughter's life, at least he could keep an eye on it. But keeping an eye had not been enough.

Back on that old bench, late in the afternoon, napkin spread on his knees, Hamilton unwrapped a juicy, dribbling hamburger and tasted a huge bite. He was glad he had returned here to eat his dinner even though a few hours earlier this spot had brought back some painful thoughts. But it was still beautiful there; calm, cool, and peaceful. Too bad he couldn't just live here in this little beachside space, become a bum and sleep nights on that very bench with *The Crest* spread on top of him for warmth.

"Ha, what a thought. The only time that paper ever warmed a cold night was when I stuffed it in the fireplace to get the wood started." He spoke out loud, that journalist's trait still very much a part of his character, and bit angrily into his burger.

"Ah, but there were some great stories . . ." He let himself wander back over the sixteen years he had spent on *The Crest,* sipping a cup of hot, black coffee and stuffing the greasy paper from the burger into a brown paper bag.

There had been the time the old bath house had caught fire in the middle of a cold, winter night and half

117

the town had stood in ice-covered nightclothes and watched the firemen desperately fight to keep the flames from reaching the boardwalk and its summer homes and hotels. Ham got one hell of a story, perched as he was on the top of a hook and ladder, scribbling bits of shouted dialogue from the firemen as they went about their jobs aided by his strong back and powerful arms when they needed an extra man.

And there was the day the Langley triplets were born—smack in the middle of the longest hospital strike the town had ever seen. With exhausted doctors working overtime to compensate for the lack of aides and nurses and well-meaning townspeople bumbling their way through first-aid procedures, Ham had found himself recruited from his position on the sidelines to help in the multihour labor and birth of the three daughters. He had been so tired by the time that day was over he forgot to take pictures and had to go back in the middle of the night to snap the sleeping trio in their cribs behind the protective glass of the nursery.

His memory on a roll now, Ham stretched back on the bench and watched the sun prepare for bed. There had been some terrific stories in that little town. And he had covered them all. From multiple births to five-alarm fires, Ham Arnold had been there, notebook in hand.

There had been crime in that seaside town, too, long before the event that shook his life to its foundation and rocked the town to its core. It hadn't been as much as one got to see on a major paper in the big city but plenty to keep an old journalist busy. Burglary topped the list with the bored teenagers of summer residents embellishing their stereo and petty cash collections with portable items from the better homes in town. Joyriding in stolen cars ran a close second on the crime scale and there had been an occasional rape and mugging on the boardwalk late at night during Hamilton's tenure on the paper. But these were usually transients—not even overnighters, and rarely stuck around to follow through on a complaint, no less give an interview to the local paper. Then, right up there at the top of the list was the most devastating, hair-raising, mind-boggling crime that town had seen in its more than seventy years on the map. The one that had ended Hamilton's career.

"Unfit to stand trial by reason of insanity . . . of insanity . . . of insanity . . ." The words echoed in Hamilton's head as the pounding of the surf brought him back to the present and he shivered a little in the chill air that drifted in off the ocean. Even after four years he still recalled those words with shocked disbelief. As for his own part in covering the trial, that had its painful elements, too. In the sharp light of hindsight he knew he had had no business attempting to cover that story. It wasn't long before the secret he had kept for thirty-five years was known by the whole town.

Running on no sleep and little food, spending every waking moment in the courtroom and searching for a way to prove Alden guilty of first-degree murder, Hamilton Arnold had been approached by a group of *Crest* staff members, who, quietly but firmly, requested that he remove himself from the position of publisher/editor. Too tired to argue with them and too beaten to find any convincing words to defend himself, he agreed to their request and removed himself as head of the paper.

All that talk earlier with his barber, Nate, about the mental hospital had sent Ham's mind on this precarious roller coaster to the past and he now spread his arms along the length of the wooden bench at the edge of the boardwalk and tried to divert his thoughts. Far in the distance he imagined he could see the sand-colored state mental hospital, could hear the "clink" of iron gates and the "click" of closing padlocks. He shook his head, rubbed the back of his neck furiously, missing the unruly curls that Nate had earlier shaved off.

What the hell was he still doing in this place, breathing that healthy air, running his hand through one of Nate Miller's prize haircuts, holding a rumpled copy of *The Crest* he had picked up from the bench? Damned if he knew. But something told him his business in that town was not yet over. And a wily, quick smile flashed on his seasoned face, banished the past, and took control of the future. With a sigh, Hamilton crushed his coffee cup and tossed it over the railing onto the sand below.

The paper cup landed softly in the moist sand and was immediately taken by the wind and carried down the beach a few yards. Alden watched it from his sheltered spot beneath the boardwalk. He was tired. His hand hurt and he didn't feel much like taking pictures this evening. His camera hung limply around his neck, unusually off center from its regular spot below his armpit. The day had passed in a painful blur of memory and reality. His mind ached and his legs were sore from running. He thought back to the events of the morning at the supermarket. All he had wanted was a jar of instant coffee.

It was almost dusk. Pink-orange wisps of sunlight danced on the sand and it sparkled. The paper cup at rest just inches from his toe. A sudden impulse. A kick. The cup flying out onto the beach. Lazily Alden got to his knees and, careful not to let his camera drag in the sand, crawled out from his hiding place under the boardwalk. He reached the cup, played with it for a few seconds, then threw it as hard as he could toward the ocean. It fell short. "Oh, shit . . ." Sand in his cut. It would start bleeding again. He must wash it off. Salt water would sting but it would also heal. He rose to his feet.

Above him Hamilton Arnold was getting ready to go home. He stuffed the brown bag with the remainder of his dinner into a wire wastebasket at the edge of the boardwalk and stopped to lean on the railing and survey the beach a moment longer before walking back. So, he wasn't the only one who liked to spend solitary time on the sand, communing with the sea. There was a man out there, a man bending over the easy surf and rinsing his hands.

"I wonder if he just had a greasy hamburger too?" Ham smiled.

Alden turned, his camera catching the final rays of sunlight and sending off sharp sparks into the approaching night. He wiped the salt water from his hand and held the camera up to his face, measuring the distance he would walk back to his room. On the boardwalk a few yards off a man watched him. Alden began his trek along the sand, winding closer to the boardwalk with every step yet keeping a steady angle between himself and the curious onlooker.

Hamilton squinted. He leaned far over the railing and shielded his eyes with his hand. It was nearly dark though, and he wasn't sure. He turned to walk in the direction of the other man, following him, conscious of a growing tension that always meant something was about to happen. He trusted that instinct and let it guide his steps. The man was leaving the beach now, climbing the ramp to the boardwalk a block ahead of Ham, heading for the row of rooming houses that lined the beach. Ham walked faster. He got to the point where the man had left the boardwalk, turned, and reached the bleached, unevenly patterned concrete himself, now only a few yards behind. The man turned into one of the houses, which one Ham was not certain in the darkness. He slowed, crossed the street to view the whole row. On the porch of the corner house, watching, blocked by a wooden pillar, his camera dangling in front of his chest, Alden puzzled. A car passed, its headlights brightening the porch. He moved forward, his camera leading. Paused. Another car. Brighter this time. Screaming headlights. Ham stepped toward the house, stared. Alden slipped quietly inside.

Hamilton Arnold waited a full two minutes before entering the rooming house after Alden. The lobby was empty and a big, old wooden ceiling fan circulated the dusty air and provided a dull buzzing sound that cut the bored silence. Ham approached the desk and struck the bell next to the register with his fist.

"I'm comin' . . . I'm comin' . . . blasted people can't remember their keys." The manager came from his room behind the wall of mailboxes and angrily took a pair of wire-rimmed glasses from his breast pocket, fitted them to his face, and peered at Ham. A smile broke out. "Well, I'll be. Haven't seen you around this part o' town for ages. Arnolds, wasn't it?"

"Arnold," Ham corrected, returning the smile. "Hamilton Arnold."

"Well, sir. What c'n I do for ya? You want a room?" The question was asked more for himself than for Ham; surely a man like this could do better for himself than a rotting old seaside hotel.

"Nope. Thanks. I've still got my little place over the other end o' town." His reporter's instincts returning, Hamilton took on the man's mannerisms and speech style just slightly—enough to convey simpatico but not so much as to condescend. People didn't call him "Ham" for nothing! "You can do me a favor, though. That is if it's no bother."

"No. No bother at all. What c'n I do for ya?"

"That fella that just came in a few minutes ago. Right before I got here. You know the one . . . tall guy, kinda skinny, messy hair . . . carries a camera." This addition brought a glimmer of recognition to the manager's face. It quickly turned to a frown.

"He's a strange one, he is. Wha'd'ya want with a guy like that? I stay clear of 'im, m'self."

"Oh, nothin' special. He just looks like someone I used to know. Wouldn't happen to know his name, would ya?"

"Nope." The manager watched Ham for a reaction. Deadpan.

Irked, he dangled the carrot himself and bit. "Might be here on th' registry." He pushed a long sheet of paper on a clipboard across the counter, keeping one hand tightly over the few names at the top of the list.

Ham didn't move. "You think I might take a look at that?"

"Wha'd you say you was lookin' for?"

Ham smiled. And smiled. The manager smiled back, nervously.

"The list?" Ham prompted.

"Oh, yeah . . ." The manager ran an ink-stained finger down the six or seven names on the piece of paper. "Here it is . . ." He looked up at Ham. "You believe this? Calls himself Smith. Mr. Smith." The manager cackled.

He took a few steps forward, smiled at the man again. Yes, there it was, printed neatly in dark letters: "Mr. Smith." The man laughed again.

This time Ham joined him—dry, soulless laughter. He paused. "Some guys think they can get away with murder, eh?"

"Sure do." More laughter, this time alone.

"But he couldn't fool you, could he?" Ham asked, watching the man's eyes.

The laughter stopped. "No sir." He returned Ham's stare in full. "Couldn't fool me."

"You've been very helpful." And Ham was gone.

A few steps from the second-floor landing, hidden in the dark recess of the curved staircase, Alden crouched, listening. Puzzled. This wasn't the man he had seen with the family. But he knew he had seen him somewhere before. Alden chewed it over in his mind for a few minutes, framing and setting his recollection of the man's face in the shadows on the boardwalk and trying to place it. It was no use. It was always that way with his memory—when he needed it, it failed him. When he shoved it away, it attacked him.

Tired and worn out from that dreadful day, he thought of sleep, of settling back into that warm groove on his bed, gently placed between the dulled marigolds and green leaves on the spread, and trying to rest. He remembered how the day had begun—with too much sleep. He clicked off the events of the night before, felt for the rough coating on the scratch on his hand in the dark. No. He would stay awake. Quietly he drew himself up to his full height and peeked around the curve in the banister to view the lobby. It was empty. He cradled his camera to him and turned toward his room. Faced a dark, wood-paneled wall and stopped as he recalled it—another paneled room brightly lit and crowded with gawkers, his trial—the moment of ultimate shame when strangers presented pictures of the work he had laid out and he could not counter with work of his own, the miracle, now faded and failed, whereby he had sought to cut directly into the imperfect human feature, correcting it as only photos in a laboratory, carefully cropped, could be corrected. His failure only increased his desire to regroup and reshoot the sequence until it was right.

But there it was, the face he was searching for—springing out from those wood-paneled walls and causing a chill in Alden today not unlike he had felt the first time he saw it four years earlier. Then the man had screamed threats and raised a powerful fist before they dragged him from the room, still screaming incoherent words about murdered grandchildren and his beautiful, little girl. Back in the dampness of the hallway Alden moved carefully toward his room and reached out to unlock the door. He had recognized the face and been able to place it but he did not know the man. All he knew was the feeling of danger that clutched at his throat.

Outside on the beach, shielded by the bulk of the big house from the bright moonlight, Ham Arnold watched the upper floor for signs of life. There. A small light illuminated a corner window, a man's shadow passed before the flowered drape. Ham stood looking up at the window for a short while, thinking. A reddish glow tinted the far corner of the big building and Ham shifted his weight to observe the side of the house. A small window, covered with black paper, emitted a thin trace of red light from around its edges. Ham leaned forward again. The corner window was still lit. He measured the distance with a trained eye. Probably a bathroom window, he thought, twisting back to watch the red frame on the tiny window. He checked his watch, glanced again at the upper window, thinking that the man had not seen him and, even if he had, could not possibly have recognized him, and headed home.

Chapter 8

IT'S finally over."

It was a litany Alison repeated frequently and with desperate intensity as a series of days with no new postcards became a full week of relief. She alternated this determined phrase intermittently with the same words voiced less strongly, accompanied by a question mark. It was when asking the question, and receiving stony silence from James in response, that she took it upon herself to proclaim it finished, clearly and vociferously as if by sheer volume and repetition she could make it so.

James knew differently. He had his own litany to contend with—silent, internal, tinged with despair. "Why," it began, "did the cards stop coming as soon as a post office box was obtained? And what would the next move be?" It was a sadistic game James played with himself, repeating these questions over and again until they left ruts in his tired mind. But it was a game he felt compelled to play—a game he somehow knew he would soon be playing against an all-too-real and deadly opponent.

For as the pattern of cardless days became apparent, it became clear to James that this pause was most dangerous. Soon, quite soon, he knew, their tormentor would strike. Clearly, they were being watched.

Here was a creature who knew their every move, who doubtless heard the sound of their voices when they spoke and planned their days out with them; watched them turn in worn and frayed at night. A tireless observer who delighted through the lens of his invasive tool in their squabbles and brawls as the ties that held them together as a family grew progressively frazzled.

All of this, James kept inside himself. Alison, too, despite her Pollyanna phrases, cringed inside, avoiding conflict with her husband whenever possible and at all costs. They barely talked anymore.

Habits, routines, and patterns were things of the past having been replaced by the neurotic idiosyncrasies of unbridled fear. James spent his nights curled in a blanket at the base of the huge bay window in the dining room, a flashlight and kitchen knife by his side. Daily, upon awakening from inevitable slumber, he would berate himself and all others within earshot for allowing him to depart from his vigil for a moment's time. Alison, too, was sleepless but alone, upstairs, in their bed. Maud slept, fitfully, under the watchful eye of Beth who had taken to sitting up with her younger sister until the latter was sound asleep—protection for Maud, she called it. Fear of falling asleep, her mother called it. They spent each day and night like this, knowing, each in their own special way, that soon something would happen to change them again.

"Mom . . . hey Ma . . . what's this?" Maud pointed to a rolled piece of yellow paper sticking out the mailbox.

Alison felt a chill pass over her, calmed it. "It's probably nothing, Maud. Just a flier from the supermarket or something." And she went over to the box to remove the roll of paper. In harsh black lettering an announcement read: "Come in for your free cut and shampoo . . . Girard's new 'Set and Style' salon on

Fifth Street—Grand Opening Today. Offer good only with this ad. Expires September 30." Alison smiled at her own foolishness, crumpled the paper into a ball, and tossed it at the garbage cans. It missed and she went over to retrieve it, stuff it inside.

"Ma . . ."

Alison recognized something wrong in the tone as soon as she heard the word.

"Ma . . . Ma . . . Ma . . . Ma . . ." It verged on hysteria.

Alison raced toward the front of the house, caught Maud coming toward her, and grabbed her. The little girl's face was white, pasty, and filled with terror. Alison knew immediately what had happened. She pushed Maud back from her a few inches and took the tiny pile of postcards the child's hands held. New ones. Alison had never seen these before. Her knees buckled beneath her and she collapsed on the lawn, stared helplessly at the cards in her lap. Gone was the fine, subtle touch of the artist. These cards were graphic—to the point.

There was a woman . . . at least Alison thought that's what it was . . . a face, framed with soft, brown hair, the fine ends of it blending into a dark, glossy stain on the pillow beneath. One eye had been unevenly hacked from its socket and hung in sickening limbo over the cracked, bloody cheekbone. A hand clutched the paisley bedspread in ominous solitude, severed from its arm. Alison felt her eyes glaze over, her stomach heave. Slowly she turned away from the cards and bent over the lawn. She vomited.

"Mommy . . ."

Alison struggled to her feet, spoke to Maud long enough to calm her, and sent her across to her friend Lisa's. She went inside, turned blindly toward the right, and found the kitchen. Alison threw some cold water on her face and swallowed a few sips. She sat down at the kitchen table to examine the other cards.

There was another eerie, artsy one—very stylized,

128

very planned. A moonlit room, glowing darkness, the dull shine of a white headboard on a double bed. In the upper corner of the card, the glint of sharp steel almost like a perfect ray of moonlight only just the slightest bit sharper, more refined. A blade.

The third card puzzled Alison most of all. Laid out like a fine still life, it showed a child's doll, meticulously chopped into neat, orderly pieces—eight of them—lying next to a soft, large white flower that oozed sticky, red blood from its eye. For some reason this one upset her most of all and she turned it over to hide the image from sight. At first she didn't notice anything odd. A white, clean paper backing looked up at her. Then it struck. There wasn't a blemish—not a stamp nor postmark—anywhere. These cards had been hand delivered.

"Please, just do it. Don't ask me any questions now, just come right home. . . . Please!" Alison fought hard to choke down the welling panic and to avoid shouting into the phone.

"Don't do this to me, Allie, tell me what's wrong . . . it'll take me an hour to get there. Just tell me what's happened . . . are the girls all right?" James's panic picked up on hers.

"It's nothing like that, James, they're both fine. I just need you. Now. Please come home."

"It's another card, isn't it? That's it, right? He found out about the post office box and they've started again. I knew it!"

"Are you going to come home or not?"

"I'm on my way."

"I really don't know what more to tell you folks," Officer McRae began as he passed the postcards across the kitchen table back to James. "Pretty awful stuff, I'll say that."

James wanted to know what could be done.

"I hate to keep saying this to you, especially when

129

you've been dealing with this stuff for so long now, but it's the same as the last time I was here. There's nothing to go on so there's really nothing we can do!" McRae substituted a tone of authority for the feeling of helplessness and foreboding that had come over him when he stepped into the Sommers' house.

Finally it was agreed that the department could spare a man or two for a house watch possibly for forty-eight hours. At the outside. Manpower was short and, difficult as it was for the victims to understand, no actual crime had been committed here. Yet.

Worse still was McRae's testimony that, man or no man, they would never catch the guy that way. "Soon as he sees anything suspicious—and these guys can tell an unmarked car from blocks away—he'll be long gone. Types like this may be crazy but they're also smart when it comes to getting caught."

It was last-ditch, a feeble attempt on the part of the officer who felt strangely drawn to these people, unhappily mesmerized by the subtle, hypnotic delicacy of the sick photos—the potential of a hot, juicy crime to solve all on his own. He offered them an idea.

"Go and get yourself one of those little bicycle bells," he told them, "you know, the kind that sell for two-ninety-eight at the toy store. Hook it up just inside your front door here and run a string back to the mailbox—underneath and through the back so he can't see it—and attach it to the lid here." He walked toward the front door, opened it, and leaned out. Pointed. "Let me show you . . . right here. Then, when this guy tries to leave another postcard, the bell will go off and you'll be able to get a look at him. It's a pretty low bell so he probably won't hear it and won't get spooked. If you get a clear description, we can draw up a sketch, put a couple of men on it, check out the neighborhood . . . like that. Just don't try to do anything on your own like running after the guy. Leave that part to us. Sooner or later we'll get him.

But it would sure help a hell of a lot if we knew what this guy looked like . . ."

The bell tested out perfectly and both James and Alison felt the slight relief that doing something—anything—in the face of a hopeless situation can bring. Both knew deep down inside that it was futile.

The game of cat and mouse went on. Sometimes, as when Beth accidentally knocked the recipe book over and found all the carefully buried cards in their separate berths, it was externally prompted—the cards prodding and nudging them further apart and into their distant, protective shells even on days when new ones were absent. The bell on the mailbox remained silent; the steel rectangle outside their door empty.

Choreographed deliberately by this self-proclaimed planner of their existence, daily life fell into a predictable, tiresome cycle. There was the daily attempt at cheerfulness, the stab at making it all go away. Also, there was the inevitable fight—varying in intensity in direct proportion to the number of hours of sleep the participants had. Meals came and went uneventfully, the food somehow finding its way to the plates and into their stomachs. Appetites were small, though, shopping trips to the supermarket markedly reduced in frequency. The eye of the omnipresent watcher was on them even when they were alone. It was like a game in which only one participant possessed rules—the first being that those rules were ever-changing.

It was the waiting that was the worst part.

Alison fussed over her special creamed chicken like a master chef, chopping onions, celery, carrots, and tiny, white potatoes into neat heaps and separating them on the hard, butcher-block chopping board with the edge of her light-wood-handled, stainless-steel meat cleaver. She sliced the chicken into small pieces and added them to the colorful mass of raw food on the board. Chopping, stirring, slicing—it kept thoughts at bay. Her sauce was almost ready. She slid the short distance from the work space to the stove and lifted the lid on the saucepan, stirred slowly with a long, wooden spoon. The phone rang—didn't it always—and she turned the flame low while she went to answer it.

"Beth . . . *Beth* . . . telephone." She listened for her daughter's voice, hung up, and returned to her sauce. A few more delicate swirls with the spoon and she ladled it into a deep casserole dish and swept the meat and vegetables off the chopping board and into the dish. She blended them carefully into the sauce, put the cover on securely, and put the dish into the oven. The timer was set for forty minutes.

Alison took her soft yellow sponge and wiped the kitchen table, put place mats all around, and took her flowered stoneware from the cabinet above the sink. She set the table absentmindedly and went to the fridge to get the lettuce, tomatoes, and onions for a salad. Next she washed and cut the salad, oblivious to the timer ticking away on the stove. The sudden "riiiiinnngg" of the bell startled her and she reached quickly for a potholder, opened the oven, and checked her dinner. Perfect. She took the hot dish out of the oven, set it on the counter, and closed the door. The switch went to "off" and she set her potholder on top of the dish, reached for a second one to lift it easily to the table. Her salad was nearly ready. She tossed the vegetables in a collander for a few seconds, dumped them into a wooden salad bowl. Ahead of her a few inches, a loaf of fresh French bread. She reached for it, tore off the wrapping, and sliced a dozen neat wedges, slipped them into a wicker basket. It was ready.

"James . . . Beth . . . Maud . . . dinner's ready." She took a potholder in each hand, lifted the casserole, and turned to carry it to the table.

"Ohhhhhhhh . . ." Her hands flew up to her face in shock and disbelief.

"Crash." The dish splintered on the floor and painted the chairs, cabinets, and Alison's espadrilles and tan slacks with gooey cream sauce. James and the two girls rushed in.

"What happened?" At first nothing was clear. The potholder must have slipped. The dish was too hot to hold.

Alison managed to point a trembling finger at the neatly set dinner table and three pairs of eyes followed its path, cautiously.

It was propped up plainly in sight, facing the sink where Alison had stood working for more than forty minutes. Stuck securely between the napkin rack and the salt and pepper shakers it seemed to leer at them, challenging. A young, naked torso, tiny breasts just beginning to rise from baby-soft skin. A dark, vile-looking seam carved just the slightest bit unevenly between them. Glossy, finely printed, carefully plotted work.

It was the twelfth postcard.

Chapter 9

A sharp pain shot through Alison's right arm and she traced its origin to her tightly clenched fist strangling the slim, white phone receiver as she listened to more platitudinous rhetoric from Sergeant McRae. Here she was being lectured—interrogated it almost seemed—on her lack of precaution at having left the back door unlatched—a rather common occurrence until recent events made locks and keys a part of everyone's consciousness. She had slipped back momentarily to the time when one could, without fear, leave a door unlocked at six in the evening. But now it was her fault. Funny how every time any one of them erred on the side of normalcy lately they became the villain. How easy it was now to blame any small act—a window left open a crack, a wrong number inadvertently given the family name, an unlocked door—for the entire string of happenings that persisted in drawing tighter and tighter around them.

And now here was Sergeant Hal McRae schooling her on basic home safety precautions, implicit in his carefully chosen words the accusation that this latest incident was wholly her fault and therefore had been avoidable. She fought him, tearing verbally through the phone lines to try and elicit some spark of empathy from this bureaucratic soldier while he, on his end, felt her drawing from him the feeling he had hidden so well—the mysterious tie he felt to this case, undefined and totally extraordinary.

He told Alison once again that he could do no more than he was already doing. The men who had watched their house for forty-eight hours had seen nothing; no description existed of the sender of the cards which were always meticulously devoid of his fingerprints, and the police were at a loss as to how to proceed next. As she heard the words rephrased to tell her the same thing they had three times before Alison felt like she was sinking in quicksand and someone was standing on the shore above her yelling that she couldn't be resuscitated until she went completely under. If only she could put a face—a name—something to this mysterious creature who had been tormenting them all month—then she'd have someone *real* to vent her anger on, to be furious at. She stood in the hallway next to the telephone for half an hour, maybe more, after hanging up on the exasperating McRae, ready to scream at everything and everyone that dared flaunt imperfection at her. There was no place for her to go, nothing to do. The girls were safely ensconced in their room and James had reluctantly gone to work. She needed to go out for a few things but couldn't bring herself to leave the house. And that only made her anger worse.

A sudden sound at the front door jolted her and she tore it open, sending James flying in the hallway. Almost before he righted himself she was on him about McRae. At last, she had someone tangible to let her frustration out on. James stood surprisingly calm in the face of the barrage she let forth and waited, exceptionally patient, for her to run out of steam.

Gently, as if offering her a sacred gift, he pulled a small, felt sack from his breast pocket and passed it to her. Fatigued from the lengthy, exhausting phone call and her high-pitched repetition to James a few moments earlier, she took it, questioning him with her eyes. Her hands dropped a notch under its unexpected

135

weight. Setting it on the phone table, she pulled the light drawstring and slid the felt bag off the object within. A gun. Steel black, .38 caliber.

Instantly alert, her brain clicked away, bringing to her mind whole pages of unintentionally memorized antigun statistics from the many leaflets that regularly found their way under their door. She poured it all from her, suddenly, hysterically, panicked by the deadly presence of that stark, black weapon. Spewing it out at James verbatim, all the deadly numbers, human accidents, personal experiences of gun victims, everything.

It would fire accidentally. James would hear a noise, use the gun in panic—kill one of them. Or himself. An accident. One of the girls could find it. It could be taken from them and used in retaliation by an unarmed interloper unexpectedly seduced by the sight of it into a more violent move than he'd planned. It could be stolen and used to commit a crime far from but not totally unrelated to them. An innocent bystander could be injured or killed. They would be liable. It could go off by itself . . . her list went on and on.

It was unclear to James just when he began to believe her tirade to be aimed at him rather than the small, L-shaped piece of steel on their hall table. Perhaps it was when she began, with all good intentions, to compare him with their malignant observer, to explain why, should a confrontation arise, he—the lunatic who stalked them—would have the upper hand. It was, she explained, because he only had *himself* to think about while James had all of them on his mind. But this his ego deleted and he felt belittled by her example, stained by this unfair comparison to a madman that left the latter with the upper hand once again. Could he not, in his wife's eyes, manage even to retain control over something as insignificant and inanimate as a handgun? Had he become so impotent in every facet of his life, in her eyes?

True, anger had robbed him of his desire for sex of late but he had ignored this, as had Alison, in the face of all other happenings, relegating it to what he knew to be its proper place alongside other forgotten pleasures that would resume when their lives did. But here was this gun, swelling menacingly into an immense symbol of his masculinity beyond all logic and believability and totally out of his control. He reached for it, slid a tight, hard palm over its surface, clutched it to him. It was reflexive. Protective. He held it out to her, forced her hand over to it, stroked it with her fingers, now sensing the full sexual implications of the weapon and of his action. She cringed, repelled by its coldness, drew away. He persisted. She had to learn to use it, to understand how it worked. He demanded it from her and she watched him, probing. She must have some means of protection when he was not home, he told her.

"So that's what this is all about." At last there was something she could latch on to, safely verbalize. "This whole thing is just a ruse to camouflage your real reason. It's all a conscience saver so you can blithely go off to work every day knowing I'm safely armed to the teeth at home. Well, I won't use it! I don't even want to know where you keep it. Put it away and don't tell me. I want nothing to do with this gun!"

He pressed it hard, squeezed it to him. Finally, exploded. "Okay, terrific. So don't learn how to use the gun. You don't ever have to see it again. But don't just stand there and lay this whole thing off on me and then when I go out and at least try to do something concrete to protect my family, turn around and say you don't want to have any part of it. Just what the hell do you plan to do the next time this guy pays us a personal visit? Invite him to have dinner with our two children and hope he isn't really a dangerous psychopath? Well?" he bellowed at her. "Answer me. You

137

won't have anything to do with the goddamned gun I bought, so what the hell are we supposed to do? Huh?"

"Daddy! What's going on? Why are you fighting again?" Beth shielded Maud with her slim body as the two hung over the banister of the staircase and peered down at their angry, red-faced parents. Alison glanced quickly from their concerned faces to the black piece of steel on the hall table and wondered if she could cover it with her hand and slide it out of view before they noticed. It was too late.

"Wow . . . where'd you get the gun? Is it real? Can I see it?" And she was down the stairs in a flash, forgetting about her younger sister for the moment.

"No you may not." Alison was first to reply and it was firm, unequivocal. "You may not see it, you may not touch it, and neither one of you"—she looked pointedly at the younger girl, still lagging back on the steps—"is ever to talk about it again. Understand?" It was Alison's own fear that prompted the declaration rather than any sense of concern she received from either of her daughters. In fact, Beth seemed down-right fascinated with the gun (an element that truly frightened Alison) and Maud was strangely quiet, also a rare occurrence.

"I'm sorry," James interrupted, "that you had to hear another fight between your mother and me, Bethie, but we all know the stress we've been under in this house and it's starting to get to us. Now I don't want you two to be frightened by this"—he reached for the gun and held it out so they both could look at it, despite a warning glance from Alison—"because I bought it to protect us, not to harm us. The main thing to remember is that neither of you is to ever touch it for any reason because it's very dangerous, okay?" He looked from each girl to the other, waited for a reply.

"Daddy . . ." The little girl was tentative, hushed, still cringing back on the steps as if afraid, not only of

138

the gun, but suddenly of her own parents. "Are you and Mommy going to shoot each other next time you have a big fight?" James's mouth fell open and he caught the gun just as he was about to drop it to the floor. He passed it to a dazed Alison as both their eyes filled with tears and they rushed together to Maud's side and smothered her with hugs and reassurances of their love and trust for each other, no matter what.

A moment later, when all three emerged for air, tears forgotten in remembered smiles, it was Beth who voiced the sound of reason. "Why don't you guys just put that thing away someplace and let's eat. I'm starved." And Alison gave the gun to James with a tremendous feeling of relief that the air had been so thoroughly cleared. As he took the gun up to their bedroom to tuck it away safely, he put an arm around Maud and explained to her calmly why he had bought it and how he hoped it would never, ever have to be used. As Beth bounced into the kitchen in search of a snack Alison leaned on the banister and watched the retreating figures of Maud and James. She never told him that she had once learned how to fire a gun and had done so many times, albeit with blanks, during a photo session some seventeen years ago. If it became necessary, it was a technique she was certain she would easily recall.

Hamilton Arnold was beginning to get into the rhythm of following Alden and starting to feel like his life once again had purpose. It took a while to regain the talent he had once had for dogging people, but once found he grew comfortable with it quickly, soon giving in to the thrill of the chase. He wasn't quite sure yet why he was so ardently following the younger man, only that they had unfinished business between them and that, this time, Ham would be sure to tie up every loose end. A man of strong will, he had virtually banished the images of his murdered daughter and grandchildren from his mind and had set his course straight and steady in the footsteps of Alden Smith. Still firm in his belief that somewhere there was hidden a piece of solid, undeniable evidence that would prove Alden Smith to have premeditated his actions, Ham felt that by following him he would, at best, be led directly to that proof and, at worst, make the other man very nervous.

Though he took the necessary precautions to avoid detection, Ham somehow sensed that Alden knew he was there and tacitly accepted it. For days his comings and goings had been lazily uneventful but, like a patient fisherman, Ham knew better than to get impatient and give up. If Alden did not know he was being followed, then sooner or later he would make a mistake, a move that would lead Ham where he wanted to go. If he was aware of his newly acquired shadow, then it would just take a bit longer. Ham's unchanging strategy remained as it was in the old days—be consistent in your moves and let the other guy make the mistakes. And so he kept on following Alden Smith. Each time he left his rooming house, went to the store, walked along the boardwalk, stopped to take a picture, Ham was right there, just a few yards behind him. All Hamilton needed was for Alden to make just one tiny mistake—anything—and he would have him. Sensing more and more that Alden knew he was being watched, Ham became a bit more brazen, took on a slightly cavalier attitude, hoping to spark an error in his opponent's game.

Even if Alden knew he was being followed, Ham was certain he did not know why. Perhaps he recalled that Ham had nearly slugged him at the trial, perhaps not. The man had been pretty spaced-out back then. But now Ham detected a sense of vigor and purpose in his quarry that had not been present in the near-catatonic figure at the defense table four years ago. It didn't really worry Ham—intrigued him, maybe—it just made the chase more interesting. He knew with absolute certainty that a man as habitual and obsessive as Alden Smith would have secreted away some solid evidence of his crime—some way of proving to *himself* what he had done, some kind of self-paid homage to his deed and a private source of reprieve from the years spent in an institution. And Ham would find it. In fact, if he played his game right, Alden would take him right to it.

Plotting each step carefully, he noted Alden's every move and habit, detailing each in hieroglyphic short-hand in his ever-present notebook. "A man of ritual, of exact duplication, a man who never veers from the straight course he sets for himself." Ham had written, "One who despises disorder." Ham had him pegged pretty good.

The first morning after his discovery of Alden, Ham had begun his research, refreshing his memory with small details that might prove necessary. An old suit-case full of clippings was Ham's library and he read through the scores of stories written on the pretrial hearings—the earlier stories written by him, others by a string of different reporters—and the psychological profiles he had conned from a police contact. Headline after headline was imprinted on his brain forever but he read on, searching for the minutiae even his mind had failed to retain—carefully, painfully avoiding even the thought of that one, blazing banner story, those three smiling faces in the photos dug out of the news-paper morgue, that single, stabbing news story that broke it all wide open and with it, tore a huge hole in Ham Arnold's comfortable, self-satisfied life.

Satisfied at last with his refreshed picture of the details of the past, no longer clouded with his interpre-tations or speculations, he set out to learn what the articles could not impart, the story of the past four years of Alden Smith's life. He phoned the hospital for an appointment that very day; showed up promptly at three to meet with the institutional bureaucracy.

"Well, well, well. Mr. Arnold. We thought you had . . . shall we say . . . passed on?" The sour mustard smile hadn't changed.

"Sorry to disappoint you." The office was the same, too. Dark, musty, stale. That tantalizing bit of sunlight slipping through the steel mesh, brightening the paper-laden wooden desk.

"Oh, on the contrary. Things have been rather . . . dull around here since you stopped . . . er . . . pursuing your cause."

Ham stared at the man.

"Yes. Well . . ." He was feeling uncomfortable. Why did this furry bear of a man always make him squirm so? "What can I do to help you?"

"I understand Alden Smith was released from this hospital just a short while ago."

The smile vanished. Two sallow hands planted firmly on the edge of the desk lifted the man an inch out of his chair. "That is privileged information, sir. Privileged!"

"Bullshit! You know as well as I that you people are so disorganized around here you couldn't keep your own mother under wraps no less someone with the notoriety of an Alden Smith."

"Well!" He was insulted. "I think our time has just run out, Mr. Arnold." He rose and indicated the door.

"Now keep your shirt on. I'm not here to make any trouble for you. I've already seen Smith. . . ." He dropped the bait.

The man sat down on the edge of his chair, about to grab the hook. "You've talked to him?"

"He seems quite . . . shall we say . . . cured?" Ham mimicked the man, ever so slightly, but was careful not to answer the question with a direct lie.

"Yes." He sat back in his seat, relaxed, the hook swallowed. "Doesn't he, though? We consider him one of our finest achievements. An astonishing recovery, don't you agree?"

142

"Astonishing. Tell me, what kind of tests did you employ to check his development?" The man stiffened again; Ham let out the line just a bit. "I mean to say, he seems so stable, balanced. I'd really like to know how you did it."

"We're all trained observers around here, Mr. Arnold. Mr. Smith was cared for by some of the best on our staff. You should have seen him. Why, we've never had a more pleasant, obedient, polite patient in all my years. Tell me, why are you still so interested? Those rumors, you know, about the victims being somehow related to you . . . they were just rumors, were they not?" the man jabbed.

"Well, you know how the press is . . ." Ham disarmed the administrator with a smile. "Anyway, it does appear I was wrong about this one. I was so certain about Smith too . . . well, no need to remind you about all that, you surely won't forget what holy hell I raised around here, will you?"

"No I won't." He returned the smile. "But then, we all make mistakes, don't we?"

"We sure do." Ham stood up. "So you based your release of Smith on trained observation, behavior within the institution, good manners, things like that?"

"That's right. We are rarely wrong, you know."

"Yes. Rarely. Well, thank you for your time. You've been a big help. Oh, tell me, has Smith been in for any follow-up examinations? Like that—"

"No. We haven't heard from him in more than six weeks."

"You *do* plan to contact him?"

"Oh, Mr. Arnold. We never go after our ex-patients . . . our 'graduates,' if you will." Another sickly smile. "Once someone takes that big step back into the outside world we don't like to remind them of the past . . . you know, interfere in their new lives. Besides, we made it very clear to Mr. Smith that we'd always be here for him if he felt he needed us, and as I've told you, we haven't heard a word from him. He is well medicated, I assure you, and that should keep him quite stable."

"What if he should stop taking the medicine—what is it—thorazine?"

"Yes. Thorazine. And why on earth should he want to do that? It's what keeps him calm, makes him feel in control of his actions. Besides, I've already told you, we explained very clearly to him how important it was to continue his medicine. He was always a very obedient patient. I assure you, Mr. Arnold, there's absolutely nothing to worry about. Frankly, we're very, very proud of this one."

"I'll just bet you are." Ham extended his hand, crushed the smaller man's wiry feeler in his grasp. "I'll see myself out."

"But . . . but, sir . . ." The man rubbed his hand, called after Ham. "I'll have to have someone escort you . . . you know the rules . . . this is a top-security institution . . . you just can't walk out of here." And the man laughed, nervously.

"No?" Ham said as a guard met him and led him toward the exit.

Ham drove his old, brown Pontiac slowly back to town, frowning at the stupidity of that man, that entire place, that could let a man like Alden Smith get the best of them. Well, he wouldn't get the best of Hamilton Arnold this time, not this time. Ham tightened his hands on the steering wheel, remembering how badly he had handled his last run-in with Alden Smith. It was stupid of him to have taken a swing at him in open court like that, to open himself up to relentless scrutiny and take the spotlight off Alden. This time he would plot his moves carefully, keep his temper in check, and control his emotions until he could trap Alden for good.

He reached the turn to Oceanview and cruised over to the beachside street where Alden was living. It was late afternoon and the sun prevented Ham from telling whether Alden was in his room or not. Working on a hunch, he drove lazily down the street to the shopping strip and glided toward the end. He spotted Alden coming out of a small hardware store, a brown paper bag under his arm, camera slung over his shoulder. Ham turned the car around, followed Alden closely as he walked back to the rooming house. "He knows I'm here." Ham smiled at the discovery, as Alden's steps grew longer, his pace faster. Ham no longer had to wonder—it was clear that Alden felt his eyes upon him. "Good. Let him squirm." Ham stopped the car, got out, and went to buy a pizza. Alden turned, just a bit, to catch Hamilton's profile as he entered the shop. Quickly, he pushed for home, raced up to his room, and stuffed his purchase under the bed with his camera equipment.

This man was starting to get to him. Disrupting, disorganizing his life. Alden knew that he should recognize him, sensed that he should fear him. But he couldn't get a fix on him, couldn't put a boundary around the man so he could place him, have some control. For the past few days he had avoided Alden's camera deftly, prevented Alden from getting one sharp, clean shot. That's all he needed. Just one. Something to stabilize and possess this man by. Then Alden could think again, could go on with his plan. Now, all he could do was wait, pretend it didn't bother him, let the man know he didn't care that he was watching him, following his every move. Maybe by doing that he could trap him into making a fatal mistake. But he found that playacting didn't work; he really did care about this person who was dogging his footsteps, standing beneath his window at night, watching. He knows I know, Alden thought. That's what bothered him most. The man knew Alden saw him, made no attempt to be subtle about his actions. What was he trying to do?

Alden thought back over his life and tried to place

that tanned, strong face, that salt-and-pepper hair, the hairy, muscular arms and chest. He couldn't remember beyond that one upraised fist that had never connected. But still, Alden knew with absolute conviction that he had the upper hand, and he reached over to feel beneath his bed to make sure that his package was safely there.

Convinced that it was he, and not his shadow, that controlled the situation, he who was doing the leading and the other man just blindly following, Alden took his camera and headed for the boardwalk. Sooner or later he would get a picture of the man, just one picture, and then he'd have total control, then he could relax. Yes, sooner or later the man would make a mistake and Alden would have him. It still bothered him that he couldn't get Ham into focus, that the man somehow knew to avoid that lens like it was the barrel of a gun. He's afraid of me; Alden smiled to himself, mirroring, quite exactly, the thoughts of the other man. He will make an error, Alden told himself. And Alden would be there to capture that wrong move on film. He walked toward the hot sunset and climbed down onto the beach to watch it fade. Without turning, he knew the man was behind him, following, watching. A ripple of anxiety passed from shoulder to shoulder and faded. Alden was okay.

Ham sat on the boardwalk in his customary spot on the end-most bench and watched Alden take his ritual walk on the beach. Sooner or later he'll make a mistake. And I'll be there to catch him. Ham settled back on the bench. Something told him to avoid that camera lens at all costs, stay out of his line of fire. He wasn't quite sure why he felt this way but it grew stronger every time he saw Alden, and it wasn't just the way the other man tried to snap off a shot whenever he thought Ham wasn't looking. It was more. That camera, Ham felt, was the missing link that would absolutely prove the premeditated nature of

Alden's crime, would once and for all wipe the slate of any possibility of an insanity plea.

His thoughts wandered back to the day he had heard the uncaring judge announce, "This court, by means of a careful review of all the evidence before it and in accordance with the psychiatric reports on the defendant, finds Alden Smith unfit to stand trial by reason of insanity . . . he is ordered into the custody of the state mental facility at Barnstead . . ."

Ham couldn't believe his ears. Clearly he had misheard the judge. He wasn't saying that Alden was ill? That he hadn't been responsible for his vicious actions? But that was exactly what the judge had said and Hamilton flew out of his seat at the bench hurling epithets and spewing hatred at the defendant. Alden had simply stared, blankly, at the furious man as two husky guards dragged him from the courthouse, his quickly fickle newspaper colleagues rushing to snap pictures of his unceremonious departure.

Ham hadn't let it end there in spite of the endless queries and speculations by the press. Numerous trips to the hospital, attempts to visit with Alden (all of them failures), endless excursions to the police station, the scene of the crime, the judge's chambers, the psychiatric review panel. All dead ends. There was, they all told him, absolutely no evidence that the crime had been planned. Not a single, concrete sign that Alden Smith had done anything more than go berserk under some tremendous, deeply private, and ill-defined internal pressure. He would be punished for that but he also deserved to be treated for what was clearly a case of temporary insanity sparked, most likely, by some sort of personal domestic problem, as were most cases like this.

He bent over to tie his shoelace as his thoughts returned to the present, and as Alden tried to catch a quick round of shots with his camera. Again, he missed, and again he felt anger, frustration, and tension build up inside him. How could this man know every time he was about to take a picture? And, more important, how could he know just how badly Alden needed to have one?

Back in his haven Alden paced and paced and paced across the small room, a wall of images of that man's face blocking his vision. His camera thumped on his chest, bruising, bumping him. He took it off, raised an arm to fling it, held up, put it softly on the bed. He lay down. Back to that hearing. The trial. His mind flew to that day and he stood at the defendant's table, hearing his sentence. A noise. A commotion. He turned. There was this man, waving his arms, shouting at the judge. "He's guilty . . . I tell you, he's guilty as hell . . . he should be locked up . . . he should be put in a cage and locked up and throw away the key. He planned the whole thing, I tell you he planned it . . . and I'll prove it . . . if it's the last thing I do, I'll prove it . . . ." And the man swung out fiercely at Alden before being grabbed by the guards and carried out of the courtroom.

Funny how the whole thing came back to him now. After he had left it all behind him. Buried it. Images rose before him and he swatted at them, trying to stick to the memory of the trial, that man . . . suddenly, a sound. A "whoosssssshhhh" of a blade in motion. A "slap." Blood spurting. Gushing up in his face. He turned his head. Another image tumbled toward him. Tiny hands guarding a face. Screaming. Careless, unaimed swipes. Pieces of flesh falling and oozing into a rug. Chasing. A doll, neatly, evenly dismembered. Bloody flowers. He clutched the bedspread beneath his twisting body. Sat up. Flowers on the spread. Colored, faded. Not white . . . no blood . . . the images receded. He rose from the bed.

Fury replaced vision and he dived for the bridge table, swept his pictures to the floor. To the bureau. A drawer full of photos. He dumped it. Rummaged frantically. There must be a photo of that man . . . just one . . . one picture to establish control. He must have that picture . . . dozens, dozens passed through his hands. Not a one of that bearish face, that crooked grin. He must have it . . . he must get him in check, frame him, hold him in his hands and fence him in. Why wasn't there one single photo of that man among all these hundreds of pictures? Why? Alden was crazed, his panic in total control.

He reached under the bed, groping. There. He had it. His small, red pocket knife. He crawled toward the bridge table, anger-blinded, seething. He popped the blade from the knife. Plunged it into one, then another, then another of his pictures. Through to the rug. Tearing. Fierce, staccato jabs. More, more, more. He destroyed them. Marred each and every one. Silently they looked up at him, not screaming now, not trying to fight . . . innocent faces accepting his blind abuse . . . Alison, Maud, Beth, that other Alison-like woman, the two other little girls . . . jab, jab, jab . . . he fell exhausted on the mutilated rug, on the pile of shredded glossy paper.

How could that man have known about Alden's miracle—screamed it to the entire court—known about the replacement of order, the cropping of life— Alden's failed plan. Humiliated him like that. Aloud. More than ever he knew he had to get that single picture of Hamilton. Just one. It was essential to his sense of balance, order. The photograph meant control. It meant stability. It was static, limited, balanced. It meant peace.

He looked sadly at the mess on the floor, the destruction a few moments' lapse could cause. Vaguely, he regretted the absence of thorazine. He gathered the pieces and put them on the table. He might be able to use them later. There were still others . . . hundreds . . . he checked the pile near the bureau for confirmation. Carefully he gathered those and put them back into the drawer, fit it into its space in the wood structure, closed it. He went back to the bridge table, knelt, and caressed the wounded bits of his work.

149

"Next time it will be different," he thought. "Next time I'll get it right!" He heard his own voice, startled, and looked around to make sure it had come from him. He was alone.

Alden smiled. Stood and reached for his camera. Disorder would not control him now. He would make sure of that. Testing, a smile still on his lips, he spoke to his tattered photos, a pledge, avenging them: "Next time I will get it right!" And he turned the handle on his door, stepped outside, locked it behind him and left.

"This town sure gets dark in a hurry!" Ham mumbled to himself as he sat in his car across the street from Alden's hotel. The sun had dropped deftly into its slot beneath the horizon and immersed the beach resort in total darkness. One by one the widely spaced streetlights sputtered on and sent an orange-yellow light down the middle of the street. Sooner or later, he knew, Alden would leave that house and begin his wanderings. "Bad move," Ham chided himself out loud, thinking of how he must be frustrating Alden by letting him know he was being watched. Perhaps he had jarred the prey just enough to lead him into a trap, toward some hard, conclusive evidence that Alden was more sane than crazy, that he had planned and executed his actions four years ago just as he planned each photograph he took with that camera. Somehow, Ham knew the two were tied together. And somehow Ham was going to prove it.

His body tensed when he spotted Alden leaving the house. On a whim, Ham ducked down in the car so Alden couldn't see him. A ten-count later he rose. Alden was at the bus stop. Twice before he had taken this bus to some unknown destination but Ham had lost him on the way. Tonight would be different. As Alden boarded the bus, Ham started the engine of the old car and pursued. It was a long, boring drive but he was alert this time, waiting for Alden to sneak off the

150

bus at an obscure stop. Yes. There it was. He was making a bus change. How had Ham missed this earlier, it was so obvious tonight. The thought flashed that now, for some reason, Alden wanted his route to be known but that would imply that he was controlling Hamilton and Ham knew that just wasn't true. He had just slipped up this night and Ham had found him out. Simple as that. He followed the second bus closely. The entire trip took a good forty-five minutes, even though there was no traffic. He was glad that he had remembered to stop for gas.

A few blocks ahead the bus turned into a pretty, residential community. Soon it stopped and Alden got out, began to stroll evenly toward one of the houses a block ahead. Ham slid the gear into low, glided a safe distance from Alden. He turned a corner. Ham pulled over. Stopped the engine. Got out. He walked to the corner, edged around it. There he was. Across the street. Staring at a house. What was he doing in this nice, neat neighborhood with its trimmed hedges and manicured lawns? Wait. He was crossing the street. Ham pulled back around the corner, crouched next to his car, and peered at Alden. He was standing right in front of a house. Good. Ham would be able to trace that. Find out who lived there. An accomplice perhaps? Unlikely. But Ham would find out. He glanced up, startled from his thoughts. Alden was gone. Still crouched by his rear right wheel, Ham tried to imagine where Alden had gone. Perhaps around to the back of the house. Would he break in? Ham didn't think so. He had that camera . . . always that camera. Well, Ham smiled, at least he had been too smart to let Alden catch a clean shot of him. Something told Hamilton as long as he stayed away from that view finder he would have the upper hand, he would be keeping Alden off balance, on edge. Alden would have to wait for Ham to make a move before he could come to life. Ham grinned. What was that? A noise. Rustling. He turned, panned his eyes cautiously over the lawns and trees that lined the street to his right and to his left. Nothing. A stray cat, perhaps. He looked again. Listened. Silence. He leaned back, still squatting, against the car and relaxed, slid down on his haunches, and shook his head. This time he had lost him but the next time he would be smarter. After getting this far he wouldn't let Alden gain control. Ham was going to win this round.

The hedge rustled again, a fine "snap" of a slim branch. Ham ignored it. Then a clanking; garbage can covers knocked to the sidewalk; the quick, silent shadow of some rummaging vagabond of the night. A tawny, black cat. And, just as quick, just as subtle, a "click."

Chapter 10

IT was past two in the morning and Alison was awakened by that intuitive sense of absence one instinctively feels when the other side of a bed regularly shared is suddenly empty. She glanced toward the bathroom for some sign that James was there but the doorway was dark. Sleepily, she reached over to his side of the bed and felt fresh unwrinkled covers. He had not been to bed. Shaking drowsiness off, she slipped on a silky robe and felt her way along the darkened hall to the steps and down. The lower house was eerily lit by sheets of moonlight slipping deftly beneath and between drawn shades. The living room was empty.

At first, the dining room seemed barren too—a stray streak of white light illuminating the dining table, a blade of light caught on the armoire door. But there was something on the table that struck Alison as particularly out of place, an odd appendage quite irregular to the smooth, polished surface, and Alison approached it with cautious curiosity and an absence of fear since the object was clearly much larger than a postcard.

She shook her head in puzzlement tinged with sadness as she neared the edge of the table and gazed at the long-hidden family photo album, lying casually open to a page of photos of a much younger Beth and

153

Maud cavorting in a makeshift backyard pool in the days before summer rental at the beach. She gently reached out to the book and flipped the pages slowly, looking down with a sense of melancholy on the many years of James's work—work he had proudly showed off to friends and neighbors and had boasted of to colleagues at the university—work he had ceased talking of in recent years and had laid to rest in the hall closet, leaving the bulk of the family photo duties to Alison or to visiting friends on holidays and birthdays.

A sound interrupted her sad reverie and she turned toward the source. It was James, sitting propped up uncomfortably against the sill of the dining-room windows, his head bent forward and resting on his chest, his legs sprawling awkwardly at odd angles. An old plaid blanket usually stored in the car for outings to sporting events and picnics served as his cover and a stiff pillow from the couch cushioned his back against the wall.

It was not so much the sight of his failed vigilance and the self-reproach that would follow that disturbed Alison this particular night but a peculiar addition to this now-familiar scene that sent chills racing along her backbone and up to the base of her neck. Carefully placed in front of the uncovered dining-room windows stood a brand-new tripod on which was balanced James's favorite 35mm camera with some extra attachments that Alison knew carried expensive price tags, not the usual toys of the home photographer. There was an automatic shutter attachment like the ones professional fashion photographers use and a bulk film loader that allowed the user the freedom to roll his own film and avoid having to change rolls after a set number of prints had been shot. The pièce de résistance was a large telephoto lens that had been affixed to the camera and pointed out toward the street.

Alison pushed back the flicker of anxiety she felt at this paraphernalia and went closer to examine it and test the borders of its—and her own—reality. It was so

154

hard to accept this sudden obsessive change in James. She reached her hand out slowly to touch the edge of the lens, to make sure she was not dreaming, and jumped back, clutching her hand to her breast and holding her breath as the camera suddenly began to click off a series of shots. James awoke with a start and banged his head hard on the sill of the dining-room window.

"Damn! Al, what're you doing up? I think I got him. It was set to respond to any movement at all and he must have just passed in front of the window. Did you see anything?" His excitement took him beyond the bounds of sleepiness and away from the rising welt on his forehead. His eyes gleamed.

"No. You didn't get him. It was me. I put my hand there and it started shooting." She was too weary to even attempt to sugarcoat her confession. So he would be angry. She had grown well used to it by now. She waited.

Stunned. "It had to be him. I had it all set up. You did something to it. What did you do? Why can't you just leave things alone? I would've had him!" Alison was afraid he would start to cry.

"You really should put some ice on that." She indicated the lump on his head and he reached up to touch it, flinched, and immediately forgot about it. He went to check on the camera and to reset the equipment so that he might resume his watch. She gently put a hand on his shoulder, left it there until he was forced to stop and turn to look at her. Impatient. "James. Where did you get all this stuff, it must've cost a fortune. Why?"

"Twelve hundred dollars, if you're so interested. And you know why. I just can't sit around here night after night and do nothing. This is all he understands, so I decided to trap him on his own level. If you'd have just left me alone, I know I would have done it. Now that he knows what I'm up to, he'll never let me get a picture of him." He was pouting, a combination of

155

overtiredness and the stress of being incessantly pounded by the invisible force that had stripped him of the last shred of protectiveness he had for his family.

She tried to be calm, tender, but her nerves, too, were frayed. His futile attempt at crossing over into the attacker's territory, she felt, was even more dangerous in its subtle implications than the overt threat from outside. "Honey, don't do this to yourself. It's just what he wants—to tear us apart, drag us down to his level. Then we're even more vulnerable. Can't you see that? You can't compete with him, you'd never win." She felt like kicking herself. Always, the wrong choice of words.

"So that's it. He's stronger than I am, he's smarter than I am, God knows he's a better photographer than I am. Maybe I should just pack up and leave and he can come right in and take my place. He's probably a better lover too. Or do you already know that?" He knew it was a completely irrational thought but he just had to hurt her.

"James!" Then, trying not to escalate the fight: "You know you don't mean that. You haven't had any sleep in days. You're not thinking straight. Why don't you just forget about all this and come to bed. Please?"

"Oh, you'd like that, wouldn't you? For me to just give up, throw in the towel, admit I'm a complete failure. Well, I won't do it! I'm not going to let him win and I'm not going to let you either. I'll get this guy, one way or the other, I swear it, I'll get him!" And he grabbed the camera off the tripod and held it to him as if she would steal it from his arms.

"But you can't beat him! Don't you see that? Not this way. It won't work!" She wanted so badly to break through to him, to see his calm exterior return, to see that fire in his eyes diminish and the old James return.

"Why can't I beat him? Tell me that . . . go on . . . tell me." He started to stalk her, walking around her in tight, little circles, not yet succeeding in making her nervous. "It's because I'm a failure, isn't that right . . . a total clod, a washout." He was baiting her, pushing hard.

"No! Stop putting yourself down all the time. I'm sick of it! You can't beat him because he's insane and you're not. That's the only reason. You can't fight him on his level because his level isn't normal. If you'd just see that and stop all this, you could beat him!" His pacing was beginning to threaten her and she lashed out. "Stop circling me like that, James, you're frightening me. Stop it!" As he edged closer and closer, he raised the camera with its oversized lens to his face, and clicked off a shot. Grinned broadly. Still stalking.

She backed away, held up her hands to her face, and tried to block the lens, growing more and more frightened not of her husband but of this stranger who had suddenly taken residence in his body and was pursuing her, attacking with that cruel, Cyclops eye.

"Why don't you smile for me, Allie? Pose for the camera, move, twirl, do something! You remember, Allie . . . you used to earn a lot of money posing for people, remember? Now pose for me! Go on, smile, damn you! Smile!" And he pushed further, clicking off shot after shot, barely focusing the camera or sighting through the lens, using the camera more as a tool of his anger than as a weapon against her, never touching her except with his angry words, scaring her more with his madness than with any physical threat, pushing her backward toward the staircase. Up, tripping over her robe. Further. The ceaseless clicking. James's face separate from the camera. Letting it function on its own, watching her fear, her loss of balance, her stumbling awareness that he was truly someone to fear. Enjoying her helplessness.

The top landing. Alison bolting for the bedroom, slamming the door. Locking. James pounding on it, clicking off shots as if they were the password to the forbidden room. Then, silence. A moment. Screams.

157

Her children, yelling. He was attacking them, hurting them. Fumbling with the lock. Dashing out into the hall. To their room. Cowering there in their beds. Startled by the bright ceiling light, by their crazed father. Screaming, crying. Not sure whether to fear this man they loved and trusted or the dark, life-possessing machine he held in his hand. Hiding their faces, crawling beneath the covers. James moving closer, reaching for the blankets, dragging them from their beds. Clicking, clicking. Raving at them to pose for him. To smile. To show their faces. Faces just like their mother's face. She hit him.

It was a forceful, stunning blow powered by surging adrenaline, maternal protectiveness. A desire to knock that demon from his body and bring her James back to himself. Both hands clasped, her arms like a club. *Swat.* Against the back of his neck. He staggered. Fell forward. The camera landing on Maud's bed, she backing away from it in terror. James on the floor. Ashen. Dazed. Aware now of the lump on his forehead, the stinging pain at the back of his neck. Turning. Alison's bare feet, the edge of her pink robe. Higher. Her beautiful face. Tears streaming down. His children. Terrified of him. Mortified. He stumbles to his feet. Clutches the edge of the bed. Beth pulling back from his hand. Alison waiting. Hiding his face from her, ashamed. Heading out of the room to the hall. Quickly into the spare bathroom. A slam of the door. The lock twisted. Water running. Sobbing.

Alison comforted the two girls, sat with them until Maud had fallen into a fitful sleep and Beth assured her mother that she was fine. Alison took the camera from the edge of the older girl's bed, unscrewed the telephoto lens, carried it out of the room, and placed both on the upstairs hall table. She passed the bathroom, listened at the door for a moment, and, hearing James's sobs mixed with the sound of running water, decided to let him have time alone. Her interference would only salt his wounds.

She caught her reflection in the hall mirror as she passed, shocked at the pale, drawn, and frightened woman who looked back at her. She took a breath, passed the mirror, and went to the bedroom. Safely inside, she closed the door, thought for a second, and then locked it. Went to the bed, took her robe off, slid beneath the covers, and lay back, tense and stiff, hoping to fall instantly asleep. Sat up a moment later. Reaching across to James's side of the bed, she slid the night stand drawer open, slipped her hand inside, and pulled a hard, dark object toward her. She propped up an extra pillow, leaned back, and stared at the ceiling. Her hands gently caressed the .38-caliber pistol and she dozed, holding it to her breast.

Alden held the three-by-five photograph of Hamilton Arnold to him like a lover. He had wasted nearly half a roll of film to get this one picture developed, not a very professional thing to do though the result was worth it. He could always get more film. He might not have another chance to capture this man on film this way. It was a surprisingly good photo, considering the stealth and cunning Alden had used to get it. He didn't like to snap pictures from behind; it involved too many incalculable variables that might disrupt the form or pacing of his work, but this rare animal had been wary from the start.

Now, caged within the white trim of this small square of paper he possessed the man in a way that both scared and excited him. He studied the photograph in detail, examining every line and mark on the man's face. Moonlight flattered him and gave Ham a somewhat younger appearance. To Alden he barely appeared his sixty years. Squatting so, propped against the dark surface of his car, he nonetheless appeared fit and slim and had the tone and build of a boxer. Absentmindedly, Alden formed a loose fist with his right hand and leered at it in sadistic amusement. Blows of flesh on flesh were never his long suit. The hand, though, remained clenched as thoughts traveled from the photo in his other palm to past photos and subjects. His knuckles whitened, the skin grew tight and dry, and sinews stretched the length of his forearm. His jaw, too, clenched tight as he fought intensely to ward off another flashback. Split-second images of splattered blood, mutilated flesh, crimson-stained bedding tumbled at him. Like cobwebs they clung to his mind and blocked his vision. He reached back violently and swept them away.

Disorder. That had been the cause of it all. Loss of control. It would not happen again. This time he would follow the plan with no slips of the hand or the mind. He focused on the picture in his hand. There was the proof. An outsider, deceitfully trying to insinuate himself into Alden's carefully constructed life and corrupt it, to bring chaos to the neat, tidy package of his existence. But now, now with this speck of simulated reality, Alden had control. He traced the man's image on the picture and felt himself possess him—own him.

In Ham's photo there was form, structure, and balance. A deed done incorrectly or an action performed sloppily could be instantaneously corrected with a single "click" of the shutter. Well-trained and practiced hands could edit life into perfection and eradicate error. In his art, Alden could exist as an infallible man, while in his mind erratic bursts of disorder ran rampant. It was with his cameras that he corrected mistakes, made carelessness seem intentional and imbalance planned. Were it not for a cruel act of destiny that required him to imbibe liquid and swallow food, he would have passed through his mortal existence as a camera, his eyes forming the lens that settled and stabilized the outside world while protecting him from it. There was too much error in life, too much spontaneity. In laughter and games, in playful youth and youthful lovemaking he found his darkest anguish. A squeal of pleasure, a sigh of ecstasy, would send him plummeting into an abyss of terror like the dark musty closet of his youth where such childish bursts of emotion often saw him banished. Waves of blackness concealing indescribable, multilimbed monsters would engulf and strangle him; slimy claws would clutch and draw him into the decay of uncalculated action and hapless movement. His camera would disintegrate in one awful burst of light and he would be imprisoned forever in a jungle of loose spirit and unbounded freedom.

Sweat poured off his body and he felt his shirt sticking to his skin. He couldn't let that horrible, waking nightmare recur—not now. He looked at the picture in his hand. It was bent, the gruff, weather-worn face now cracked under Alden's pressure. Frenzied, he crumpled the shot into a ball, crushed it powerfully in his fist, and tossed it to the floor. He stamped on it. It was all his fault. He was too imperfect, he let himself succumb too often to the evil temptation of his memory. Now he would have to print another one. No, he would print dozens. Dozens and dozens and dozens. He would engulf Hamilton Arnold totally, would possess and swallow and completely digest this man until he was no longer a threat. And only then would he cut and chop and dissect and separate that image until it was perfectly, absolutely in his control and he would be ready at last to meet his subject in the flesh.

The sweat dried on his skin as quickly as it had burst forth and he went to his bathroom-darkroom to begin the task. The red bulb securely replacing the white, the door tightly closed, and the black, cardboard square firmly in place in front of the small window, he began his chore.

Hamilton Arnold was keeping quite busy himself, using up old favors and cadging new ones in his search for information on the family that resided in the house at 121 Third Street. Following Alden there the other night had only been the first step in a very long, long trek. It would not do for Ham to assume that whoever lived in that house was somehow related to Alden and his crime, an accomplice either before or after the fact. It was too tempting to think that this was possibly the hiding place for the evidence he knew Alden had secreted before returning to the scene of the crime that night long ago. But Hamilton could not simply barge in and make unfounded accusations—not yet anyway. There would be a proper time for confrontational dialogue, a time when it would serve its ideal purpose of intimidating the suspect into a confession, if need be, but that time was still far off. For the present, Ham settled into the dreary legwork so often a part of his profession.

Through careful digging, he gradually uncovered the story of the pleasant, popular, and respected family that had occupied the attractive suburban house for more than fifteen years. He learned about the man who was being groomed to take over the department chairmanship in fine arts at the local university and about the beautiful woman he had married fifteen years earlier, putting an end to her skyrocketing career as a high-fashion cover girl. They had two young girls, both with the good looks and the intelligence that ran in the family. Clearly, this was a picture-perfect, ideal American family much like a similar family that he had loved long ago. Gradually Ham's perspective changed. Either Alden Smith had a very secret, different side to his life, or these people were connected to him in only the most peripheral of ways, perhaps ones which they themselves did not even know about.

Through all of the interviews, local newspaper clippings, university bulletins, old press releases, and bios of Alison Ames, there had been one very odd and puzzling lapse—not a single clear, recognizable photo of the family together. It was a coincidence that particularly irked Hamilton because of the similarity it bore in painful closeness to that other family. Photos of the residents of 121 Third Street became his obsession and he put aside all interest in learning more about their background and current activities while he searched for a single picture. Sure, there were photos of Alison, all dressed up with formal makeup and stylized lighting, and there was the requisite faculty pose of James in a stiff suit and tie, but so far none of the two children and not a single current photo of Alison.

Ham's quest might have gone on for weeks had not the tidbit issued by a mailman piqued his interest beyond restraint and forced his hand. It was when he learned of the family's yearly excursion to Oceanview for a three-month stay in a beachfront house that his search for a photo stopped and all the bits and pieces of his investigation fell together. It didn't take more than a few phone calls for him to learn how many summers the family had spent in Oceanview or which house they had rented. For Ham, that clinched it. He marched up the front walk and rang the bell.

Once. Then again. He sensed someone looking at him from a slit in the drapes. A moment. Then the door cracking open. He smiled. "Morning, ma'am. I wonder if I might have a word with you?" He willed the door to open wider.

Alison looked carefully into the weather-worn, handsome, and powerful face that waited outside her door. There was no feeling of fear, no hint of a threat coming from this man. He looked like a friend. Still, she remained cautious. Her instincts were well worn of late. She opened the door wider.

"How can I help you?" She returned the smile, now fixed in stony silence on his face as he looked into her eyes. His pause, too long. She began to feel afraid, clutched the door, ready to slam. "Sir?"

"Huh?" It was the first time in his life that Ham could recall ever being totally speechless. It was as if he was speaking to a ghost. How could she possibly still be alive; he had seen pictures of her, her beauty hacked to shreds by that butcher's blade. But here she was. He held out his hand to touch her face, his eyes

163

glazed, almost filling with tears. A stinging, smarting pain. The door slammed hard in his face, almost catching his hand. He was jolted back. Calling to her. Banging on the door. Ringing. All of a sudden, stopping himself. God, how could he be so stupid? He must be scaring the poor woman half to death. He had never been so out of control. He looked around, half expecting a patrol car to drive up and chide him, perhaps cart him off for some ridiculous questions. The street was empty except for his old car parked on the other side. He touched the front door gently as if asking forgiveness, turned, and crossed to his car.

Alison peered cautiously through the slit in the drapes as her fingers nervously dialed James's office number. The man was leaving. He had gone across the street to an old, dark-colored car and was getting in. She took deep breaths, tried to stop her hands from trembling. Finally, the voice of a secretary. Impatience. At last, James's voice, annoyed, even before she started speaking.

"Oh, God, James . . . he was here. A strange man. He just walked right up and rang the bell and talked to me. I was never so scared in my life."

"How did he get in? You didn't leave the door open again?" There it was again, the recriminating tone.

"No. I opened it. I looked out and saw him and thought he looked okay, so I opened the door and talked to him. But as soon as he saw me he got all spooky and weird and I slammed the door in his face and he went away. He's sitting outside in his car right now."

"I can't believe you, Allie! How could you be so stupid?" Not one word of concern or worry for her safety, not one question about whether the girls had, by accident, been at home. She was sorry she had called. "You opened the door because *you* thought he looked okay. Brilliant. Great logic, Al. What do you think psychotics do, carry around business cards announcing that they're there to kill you? They all *look* okay. Geez! I don't believe it! Now, listen." He had that firm sense of control back in his voice; someone must have entered his office. "I want you to lock the doors, stay in the house, and don't leave until it's time to pick the girls up from school, you understand? Then just use the garage entrance so he can't see you until you're driving away in the car, okay? And for God's sake, Allie, don't answer the door—to anyone!"

"James." She stopped him before he could hang up on her, her hands now completely stable, her voice strong, her fear collapsed into anger. "I'm not going to be a prisoner in my own house. That's just what he wants and I refuse to let him control me that way. I have some errands to run after I get Maud and I'm going to do them. I'm not going to stay trapped like some animal in a cage." She could feel the effect her words had sizzling right back through the phone lines. Oddly, it made her smile.

"Well then, why the hell call me in the first place when you know damn well you're not going to listen to me anyway?" And he hung up.

Quietly, she went to the edge of the window and peered out from the side of the drapes. The car was gone. She took a deep breath and gathered her things together so that she could pick up Maud at school and do some shopping at the market.

Hamilton had thought better of leaving his car parked so visibly across from the house and had gathered himself together enough to move it just out of view so he could still watch without being seen. Just as soon as he turned the motor off he dug deeply into his crowded glove compartment and pulled out a cherished and now-yellowing envelope that had not been opened in four years but rather kept as a silent tribute to the strength of his memory and his love. He opened it with slightly shaking hands and spread an old front-page newspaper clipping on his knees. It was a blazing, banner headline, the one story he hadn't been able to look at, or read, since the crime. He fought back tears as he at last let his eyes look on the faces of his beloved daughter and two grandchildren, smiling up at him from that page in defiance of the brutal copy that described their deaths.

He glanced toward the direction of the house, chided himself for spooking the woman. But how could he have possibly known? Those earlier modeling photos did not do justice to the resemblance, the excess of makeup and polish, the artificial light, all contributed to masking the incredible similarity. It was like finding a missing twin. An incredible, terrifying coincidence. A frightening omen. It was as if the woman in that house being watched by Alden Smith, a woman with two pretty young daughters to care for, was his very own, beautiful young daughter brought back to life to be reclaimed, newly cherished, and finally, ultimately, protected.

He stopped his wanderings as he heard the sound of a car engine. Folded the article carefully and restored it to its hiding place, cleared his mind of any lingering fantasies that this woman was anything more than a stranger who bore a startling resemblance to his daughter and who, by the force of that resemblance, was in most deadly peril, and proceeded to follow the station wagon that pulled from the driveway and passed in front of his watchful eyes.

The supermarket that afternoon was crowded and noisy and Ham thought better of his idea of trying again to approach Alison there with his admittedly farfetched-sounding warning of the danger that threatened her and her family. He had already succeeded in frightening her, much to his annoyance, and he wanted to make this second attempt at contact one of calm, rational, detached professionalism. Hopefully, she would agree to listen to him but first he must calm and settle himself so that his approach reflected a sense of nonthreatening self-control. The crowded, noisy atmosphere of the market might allow her to make it difficult for him and then he most certainly would not get another chance. He had a better idea.

Leaning on his car he let the late September sun warm his face and kept a watchful eye on the supermarket doors. It took about half an hour but at last he saw them. They were alone, the mother and the younger girl, so much like his baby granddaughter. He couldn't miss them, they were so like twins. And so much like those other mother-daughter twins. He put the past out of his mind. Waited a moment to make sure the father wasn't with them and approached slowly, his warmest grin on display.

"Maud! Give me a hand, will you? You're the laziest person I ever saw. Grab one of those packages and give it to me!" Alison was struggling with a heavy bag of groceries as the little girl looked on, empty-handed.

"You look like you could use a hand." Ham passed the second stuffed grocery bag to Alison as she bent over the gaping trunk of the car.

"Oh." She stood up. "You again. What do you want? Leave us alone." She took the bag from his hands and held it in front of her for protection.

"I promise I won't bite, I just want to talk to you for a minute." Very calm, a reassuring tone. "Why don't you let me help with those." He reached for a third bag.

"I said I can manage." She turned to dump the bag she was holding into the trunk and noticed him smiling at Maud, the little girl eyeing him cautiously but without fear. "You stay away from her. Maud, get in the car."

"Ma . . ."

"I said move! Now." She left Hamilton holding her last bag of groceries and went to shove the lingering child into the backseat of the car.

"I want to sit in front, Ma. What's the matter with you? He's got our stuff."

"Just sit there and be quiet. Don't get out of the car.

167

Close the door and wait for me. I'll get our things. There's nothing to be afraid of."

"I'm not afraid." The child meant it. For a brief second Alison felt silly at her own behavior. But it was better to be a little foolish than to pay the price for being too lax. This man could be anyone. She turned back and took the bag from his hands, staggered just a bit under its weight, and put it into the car. Throughout all of this he just stood calmly and watched her, said nothing further, made no move to touch her or Maud, stayed physically clear of the car. She glanced quickly into his face. Still those kind lines, twinkling eyes, nonthreatening demeanor. She almost wanted to hear what he had to say.

"No!" She said it more for her own instruction than to keep him at bay. He looked a bit surprised.

"It's really very important for me to talk to you, Mrs. Sommers. It'll only take a minute. We can talk right here if you like."

"How did you get my name? Who are you?" She was frightened again, glanced nervously at Maud who had her hot face pressed to the glass and was calling to Alison to hurry before she died of the heat. Under other circumstances she would have just told Maud to open the window, sit back, and wait but right now all she felt was a tremendous urgency to get them safely home. She turned from him without getting an answer, climbed into the driver's seat, and started the car. A shadow blocked the sunlight streaming through her side window and she turned, a surge of panic lifting inside her as the strange man blocked the entire door with his solid frame and prevented her from moving the car.

"Mommmmyyyy!" Maud's pitch was rising and Alison knew tears were soon to follow. She glanced back over her shoulder and saw the look of fright on the little girl's face as the man pressed into the car, waiting. Then, suddenly, his face close to hers, sticking through the window, trying to talk to her again. Nonthreatening in tone but by the very closeness and size of his body, a danger to her in her shaken frame of mind. She turned toward him fast, practically smashing noses, and he moved back an inch, took one solid, long look into her terrified eyes, heard Maud's increasing wail, and backed away. In a flash, the car was in drive and Alison was tearing out of the market parking lot, ravaging a wire wastebasket with her right rear fender as she bumped down the driveway and turned toward home.

Ham folded his arms across his chest and watched the station wagon race away while chastising himself once again for mishandling the situation. The woman was obviously much too frightened to accept or deal with any of the information Hamilton had to impart, and had he been given the opportunity to tell it to her, chances were slim that she would have believed a word. But she and her daughter were both terribly frightened of something and, as sure as Ham was that he would have to find another way to warn them, he was equally certain that he would find out what was causing that terrible fear and put an end to it. One thing was certain: whatever it was, Ham was damn sure it had something to do with Alden Smith.

"Mr. Sommers?"

James looked up from the paper he was grading on his desk and frowned at the intrusion of the burly, salt-and-pepper-haired man.

"Mr. Sommers." He seemed to take James's stony silence as an affirmative and proceeded, "I know you don't know me but I've got some information that's of vital concern to the safety of your family and I suggest you listen." From the outset, Ham could tell he would not like this other man. He waited, blocking the door with his body, studying James's reaction. If someone had barged in on him in his private office, Ham would've thrown him out on his ass. He had a feeling James wouldn't even try.

"You just can't come barging in here, giving me orders." His anger was rising fast, hands planted on the edge of the desk, ready to spring to his feet. "Who the hell do you think you are?"

"Well," Ham tested him, softening his tone, relaxing his threatening stance, "once you've heard me out, I hope a friend."

"You're the guy who scared my wife half to death this morning trying to break into our house. You've got one hell of a nerve coming in here with some cockamamie story about my family's safety when you've been terrorizing them all along. I'm calling the police." He reached for the phone, stopped himself when the other man made no move to stop him.

Typical reaction, Ham thought to himself, a bit disappointed. He had hoped for a bit more strength in this man; he might need him if things got rough later on. Well, there was time. Besides, Ham was intrigued by James's confession that his family was being terrorized. He had to know details.

"Look, Mr. Sommers. I apologize for frightening your wife. Believe me, it was purely unintentional. And as for breaking into your house, well, I don't really think that's what she told you, is it?" James looked at him. "I didn't think so. You've a nice family, pretty home, comfortable job. I don't want to take that away from you. But I've got good reason to believe that someone I've been after for a very long time wants to do just that, and if you'll help me, I can stop him for good." Ham decided to approach James as an ally rather than an adversary, feeling it was the quicker way to gain the younger man's trust and cooperation.

"You're a cop?" It was almost a statement, as if James hoped for a positive reply, something to assure him that his inertia in the presence of this man, his inability to throw him out of his own private office, was somehow justified by superior instinct at detecting the presence of police authority.

"Reporter, ex actually. But this isn't business for me. It's personal."

"What could be so personal to you about my family?"

It was a legitimate question and Ham relaxed a bit more. The man had possibilities. "Well, it's not so much your family as the man I think is responsible for terrorizing them. Him and me have something real personal to settle."

James saw the steel in the other man's eyes and knew not to press him further. Still irked by the man's uninvited presence in the office, and angered by his own failed instincts and his lack of conviction about throwing the man out, he felt trapped by his own delay in responding and felt his body sink back into his chair. He should have thrown him out after his first words, shown him who was boss in no uncertain terms and gone back to his work. That's what he should have done. Now it was too late. All he could do now was listen. He closed the paper on his desk.

"Hope you don't mind." Damn him! He had zeroed in ffortlessly on Arthur Blackmore's carefully hidden bar and was pouring himself a glass of scotch just as if the bar had been planted right in the center of the room with a "help yourself" sign blazoned on top. James started to rise again, angered, but was suddenly overcome by a sense of exhausted amusement at the obvious skill of the intruder. "Get you one? You look like you could use it."

Out of control, James heard himself laughing and soon felt the tears fall down his cheeks as the fit brought a stitch to his side and he looked up at the solemn-faced man standing over the desk with two brimming glasses in his hands. "Here." James took the glass, had a small sip, and coughed violently. Hamilton swigged half of his, sat in a comfortable chair across from the desk, and waited. James sipped again, put the glass on the desk, wiped his eyes, and looked at his visitor. He was a kind man, at least. Not one word about James's outburst, his loss of control, inability to handle just one more stressful situation. James took another sip. Felt warm, calm. Waited. Ham finished his drink and reached toward the desk to place his glass on a blotter.

"Well, who the hell *are* you?" James spoke at last and finally received one of Ham's brilliant smiles.

"The name's Hamilton Arnold." He leaned forward, extended his hand to a surprised James, and they shook. "Okay if I call you Jim?" He didn't wait for an answer, ignored the look of distaste the name brought to James's face. He was testing the waters, wading in slowly. As brash and bold as his actions were, Ham knew that his story of the brutal and sadistic murder of a young mother and her two little girls would not be received easily by this family man, and despite his admission that his family was being terrorized, Ham doubted that anything that had occurred to date to frighten James's family was even a scratch on the surface of what Alden Smith was about to do. He stepped into the story gently.

With a newsman's clarity and brevity of detail, Ham filled James in on the basic facts of the case, leaving out only his personal reason for being involved and some of the more vicious specifics of the murders. He had brought a few clippings to offer as proof but James, accepting the story in unquestioning silence, required no documentation.

"I've seen the pictures he took" was all he said and Hamilton fairly flew from his chair to the edge of the desk and planted his face squarely in front of James in anxious, almost delirious, anticipation. He knew it! Psycho or no, Alden Smith was a stickler for detail and documented every inch of his life. For four years Ham had known that the murders had been no exception and here was his proof. It was all he could do to stifle a shout of glee and lift James from his chair.

"Where? Where are they? I must see them!"

James felt himself smile inside. At last, here was some little element of control that he had engineered, albeit accidentally, bringing himself closer to par with this imposing man. He actually knew something that Hamilton Arnold did not know. He, too, felt a shout of glee coming on but swallowed it. *They* had a job to do. Together, they would lure and trap this Alden Smith, and each vanquish his personal demons.

Slowly, not wanting to diminish the pleasure of making the other man wait for the one piece of information James coveted, he told of the postcards, dropping each one on Hamilton's eager ears just as Alden had dropped them on James the past several weeks. But it wasn't working the way James thought.

Ham was stopping him, preventing him from describing the content of the cards, discussing how each one had arrived and the way each precautionary measure was foiled. Ham wanted to see them for himself and the violent sense of urgency he conveyed to James precluded any further game playing on James's part. He made a quick, instinctive decision to trust Ham at that moment, though he already felt a growing bond from their mutual purpose. He picked up the phone to call home, determined that he would only allow Ham to view the cards if Alison and the girls were out of the house. No answer reassured James that Alison had taken Maud to watch Beth play softball; they would be out of the house for at least two hours, and Hamilton's promise that he would be in and out of the house before the family returned convinced James to share the cards with him.

Like it or not, James thought as he locked his office, they were partners. And, as he drove home with Ham following, he wondered if he would regret it. Certainly part of James accepted this partnership with a sense of relief since now his own stumbling attempts at stopping Alden would have solid backup. The rest of him, though, wanted to rebel at the invasion and barge onward by himself, damning the results.

Ham, too, accepted the partnership reluctantly, knowing that it would be futile to attempt to convince this zealous but self-obsessed man that he might do more harm than good where his own family was concerned. Ham would have to be doubly vigilant now. James was still an unknown quantity, and the very fact that he had given his trust so readily made the older man wary. Clearly this was someone who was so overstressed, so excessively tired, and so bent on being the one to save his family from harm that he would blunder into mistakes most men would easily avoid. Ham understood the protectiveness, the desire to save face in front of wife and children, and he respected it. But it was the other quality that his reporter's nose detected beneath the surface that made his skin crawl. A quality he could not yet define, only feel, a faint glimmer that told him there lay buried beneath the sensitive ego, the high intellect, the quick temper, and fast tongue of James Sommers the seeds of a violent, brutal, fiercely destructive man. A man frighteningly similar to Alden Smith.

Chapter 11

HAMILTON Arnold, true to his word, had stayed just long enough to commit each of the post-cards to memory, building up with each vivid deadly image an increasingly maniacal portrait of Alden Smith. The pleasure this conclusive documentation of the murders (and thus, their premeditated nature) brought to him was greatly tempered by the knowledge that the graphic photos implied a present and very real danger to Alison, Maud, and Beth Sommers. The detailed story Ham had told coupled with the strong visual evidence convinced James beyond a doubt that his family was in serious peril.

The solution Hamilton offered, a very complex and dangerous plan, was more the ploy of a high-stakes gambler than a man bent on some sort of personal revenge, but James sensed that Hamilton was so determined in his pursuit of Alden Smith that no plan, even a high-risk one, could fail him.

When James closed the door on the friendly stranger who would be choreographing his life for the next few days, it was with a mixed sense of relief and regret—the first at having such formidable help, the latter at knowing that he needed it. Deep inside, buried with the myriad emotions left over from the days when he was a budding photographer in love with the world's most beautiful model, was this new, slowly burgeoning sensation that had begun with guilt, fed on his insecurity, and was now gaining strength from the two outer forces that were playing reckless tug-of-war with his self-esteem and control.

Pulling at James from one side through fear for his wife and children was this invisible Alden Smith whose ego was so powerful that he could photograph the ax murders of his family with the calm eye and steady hand of a detached professional. Hamilton Arnold, so brash and comfortable that he could walk into the lives of strangers with barely an introduction, tugged at James from the other side through the threads that held his own self-image and character together. And, throughout this internal turmoil James's family was left quite alone.

"Hi, Daddy. Boy, did Beth strike out today! " Maud twirled into the kitchen in an ebullient mood reminiscent of the prepostcard days, swooped on top of the cookie jar before her sister and mother were barely in the door.

"A lot you know. I did not strike out. I popped out. There's a difference."

"Only two cookies, Maud." Alison grabbed the extra six from Maud's eager hands and put them back in the jar as the little girl grimaced with a mouthful of chocolate chips and raisins.

"Big deal," Maud was mumbling with her mouth still full. "You were still out, weren't you?" With that infallible logic, she poured a big glass of milk and washed the first cookie down in big gulps.

"God, you eat like a pig!" Beth took a small bite from an apple that she selected from the fruit basket on the windowsill.

"Do not. Pigs don't eat cookies and milk." Maud giggled, her mood not about to be spoiled.

"Well, I hope you get fat!" The two girls had been too busy bantering and too hyped up over their long and tiring afternoon at the softball park to take much notice of their oddly silent father, who was gazing pensively at a jigsaw of photographs spread out on the kitchen table. At first, Alison thought they were more snapshots from the family album and hoped that by ignoring them she might succeed in sustaining the happy mood and avoiding a scene.

From what she could see at a casual glance, they were mostly of her and the girls, though she couldn't make out the location or the poses without looking more closely. But the inevitability of an argument loomed larger when she found she could not ignore his brooding quiet, particularly in the face of such lively conversation around him. Lately, the only thing that seemed to brighten James's days was his children, and his seeming ignorance of their presence in the kitchen in spite of their light mood led her dangerously close to the edges of his recently erected boundaries.

Not wanting to involve the girls, she chose to stand quietly behind James and peer at the pictures over his shoulder rather than asking to see them and risking an unpleasant response. The photos were clearly not the memorabilia of bygone vacations and lighthearted weekends as Alison's stiffening posture quickly indicated and her eyes flicked back and forth over dozens of grossly out-of-proportion and misfocused shots of her terrorized expression and the two girls' frightened reaction to their father's mania of the other night. There were about seventy prints in all—most of them highly distorted by the oversized telephoto lens James had failed to remove before his spree. The house-of-mirrors effect the magnification had on their fright-deformed faces was insanely grotesque. There was none of the delicate, fine-boned beauty of Alison nor the gazellelike posture of Beth or the vulnerable sweetness of Maud in these photos. Taken as if from the dark side of the mirror, these were backward glances into the malignant deformities of panic and terror and the destructive acidity of emotional betrayal.

Alison wasn't sure what disgusted her most, looking at these cruel caricatures of herself and her beautiful children or knowing that James had wanted them to be developed and was now studying them with the caressing eye of an artist. Both frightened her, but it was the latter that made her bile rise, aggravated by the cold shoulder James kept turned to her in spite of her furious eyes searing into his work and his flesh. But it was the innocent intervention of Maud that catapulted the situation beyond silence when Alison stepped in to block the photos from the younger girl's eyes and James flew into a rage over her motherly censorship.

Jumping up from his seat at the table, he hurled Alison away from his photos, sending her slamming into the sink and immediately setting both girls to terrified crying as they ran to comfort their mother. Grabbing handfuls of photos from the table, he rushed toward them and stuffed the collage of pictures in front of their tear-filled eyes, forcing them to look at his "work," his "art," shoving photo after photo at the cowering mother and children.

These distorted grimaces, according to James, were their true faces. These, their valid expressions. Beauty was a lie. Fine lines, soft lips, rounded cheeks—all illusion. Alison's whole life was a lie. Her genes were a fraud. The camera told the truth and these distorted, disfigured, and demented images of their warped and outsized faces were the only valid reality. These were the images of his legacy, the testament to his family, the monument to his trampled ego and sense of self-worth. These were the real Alison, Beth, and Maud, and that which existed in the tangible, three-dimensional world of that sobbing suburban kitchen was pure fantasy. It was the flat, square, bordered, simplified, magnified, and disembodied image that represented natural perfection and James had discovered it in his pictures and had preserved it there—there; he pounded on the pictures—for them to witness and they mocked him.

He raised his hands as if to strike them violently and Alison burst out of her panic and stormed him, ripping photos from his stunned grasp and tearing them into shreds which dusted the kitchen floor. Shooing the hysterical children out of the kitchen behind her, she braced for a confrontation, felt his brutal slap across her face. Shaking her head back to banish the stinging tears, she refused to look toward her screaming children for fear they would run back to her. James was stalking her again, out of control, his eyes wild, his hands waving askew, aiming blows but not connecting, staring at her but not seeing. He turned suddenly, grabbed the kitchen table, and upended it quickly, scattering the photos beneath cabinets and shelves. Then, just as suddenly, he sat down in the center of the floor where the table had been and began to sob.

Signaling to Beth and Maud to stay back, Alison cautiously circled James, collecting his photos from their resting places all over the kitchen and stacking them neatly in a pile. Pausing for a moment, she slid down gently beside him and twisted around so that their knees just barely touched and she could see his tear-stained face. She handed the neat stack of photos as a peace offering and he merely stared, blankly, not accepting. Alison laid them down on the floor next to his right knee and sat calmly, watching him. Clearly, the anger was dissipated and only words, however vitriolic, would resolve this painful stalemate.

Gently, she asked if he had gotten any photos of their assailant with all of that expensive equipment, before he fell asleep and before he began attacking them with it? There was just enough edge to her voice to provoke him, to lift him out of the web of self-pity that had enveloped him.

"No, I didn't," he said piteously, obviously smothering in self-hatred. "I'm now a complete failure at protecting my family, that's what you're thinking, isn't it? Or should I say I'm finally a success—at failing at everything. I can't stay awake when I want to, my

179

wife sleeps with a gun next to her bed, and now I can't even get a fucking picture right. Oh, I'm really something.'' His voice dripped with loathing and pity for the man he felt he had become. It was her control over the gun that really got to him. After all her protestations about being afraid of it, she clearly saw it as of more use to her than he was.

Beth timidly poked her head in to the kitchen with Maud clinging to her shoulders and, seeing both her parents sitting in relative calmness on the floor, the photos stacked neatly beside them, felt it safe to enter. She held something in her right hand but seemed reluctant to part with it, lest it add to the anger between her exhausted parents, becoming in a sense a parent herself, in the way she chose to guard her mother and father from outside tensions and her younger sister from her parents. Alison glanced up first and saw the small, white square clutched in Beth's hand and immediately shifted her focus to the outer danger. James's glance followed hers and he, too, felt the threat of another postcard. He held out his hand to Beth, who reluctantly relinquished the card and backed away a few steps.

The back was clear white, unmarked, and blemishless. It had most certainly been hand delivered, and quite recently. Gingerly he turned the card over, averting his eyes by instinct and bracing himself for the gory sight that was sure to await him. Then, as suddenly as his anger had stopped, a roaring scream, a furious surge catapulting him to his feet, bolting from the kitchen, toppling Beth to the floor and sending Maud scampering for cover behind the fallen kitchen table; storming through the hall and up the stairs to the bedroom and a ferocious "SLAM!" as he bolted himself inside.

Alison crawled over to Beth, rubbing a sore knee and comforting a teary Maud as she groped for the postcard and steadied herself to look at it. "Boy, I don't understand what that was all about," Beth commented as Alison held the postcard, facedown. "I think it's kind of cute." Alison flipped the card quickly over, looking quizzically at her daughter for some possible explanation of her remark, then letting her eyes settle on the photo resting in her lap.

It was dark-edged, softly lit by moonlight, and quite gentle in style, unlike all the others. A mockery, in fact, as it was clearly intended to be; it had achieved its desired effect. A single, well-framed, and balanced photo of a sleeping James, his chin resting squarely on the dining-room windowsill, plaid blanket wrapped around his pajama-clad body, legs crossed beneath him on the floor. And just to his right, set slightly off center, pointing out toward the darkened street through the uncovered windows, balanced precariously on a brand-new tripod and sporting a large telephoto lens, James's favorite 35mm camera.

And as she sat holding that cruel humiliation of James in her trembling hands, that postcard that was far more vicious, more deeply penetrating than all the bloody others, for the first time Alison understood the magnitude of the threat against them. Here was a challenger so deft in his puppetry that he had his opposers fighting nearly the entire battle among themselves so that when the time came for them to face him, there would be no real fight left.

"There." Alden loved this delicate work. It challenged him, kept him thinking. He couldn't travel back when he was engrossed so in his work. That pleased him. He inched the tweezers a step closer to the photo in front of him. A conglomeration of snips and pieces of the injured photos sat in a small box to his right. To his left, a set of finished prints. Before him, nestled on a backdrop of solid black cloth, his masterpiece. A single, perfect snapshot which he embellished ever so slightly with the odds-and-ends survivors of his violent siege. Slowly, carefully, he altered the image before him and created a shockingly new, startlingly real substitute. An infinitesimal spot of glue, a speck of a past photograph—these were the ingredients of his visual recipe, and he stirred and tasted and spiced the image over and over again until it was flawless. Then, setting it lovingly against the deep blackness, he poised his box above it, neatly spaced and measured the distance and the light, and snapped the shutter.

For nearly seven hours he worked at this detailed labor, adding and deleting pieces of movement and background from a select group of photographs, replacing static images with dancing ones, illuminating darkness and shrouding light. As each new one was completed, he snapped a preserving picture, moved on to the next until his montage collection was complete. At last finished, he gathered the pasted and cut photos into a neat pile and stored them in the box with the snippets of his last rage. He fought back sleep and stiffness and opted for the tranquillity of his darkroom, the silence of the red glow, the peace of seeing new photos born. He worked through the night.

Morning found him cramped and sore in the bathtub where he had crawled for a short nap while waiting for his work to dry. He looked up sleepily at a long line of glossy, detailed work. No one could tell they had been doctored. Only the few deliberately grotesque ones showed signs of outside intervention, and then quite admirably. He felt a swell of pride as he raised himself from the tub to have a closer look. Yes, these were excellent. He had quite outdone himself.

He went into the bedroom. In front of him, papering the corner nearest the makeshift desk, a bitter shrine to Hamilton Arnold—a wall glazed with several dozen replicas of that single, night-lit, semi-full-face photo, cut up and cropped into perfection. Alden glowered at them. Counted deliberately and viciously aloud. "One, two, three, four, five, six, seven, eight, nine, ten, eleven, twelve . . . one, two, three, four, five, six, seven, eight, nine, ten, eleven, twelve . . . one, two, three, four, five, six, seven, eight, nine, ten, eleven, twelve . . ." There were six dozen prints. Alden laughed. It was a harsh, guttural, alien sound, barely recognizable as emanating from pleasure. Alden stifled it.

His plan had come off flawlessly, his dedication to order had paid off. He could move on to the next phase. In possession now of those photos, he could no longer be threatened by the man whose image he had cut and cropped into correctness so that none of the imperfect reality remained to jar him. The man could continue following Alden if he wished, but even with that shadow but a few steps behind, Alden was again alone.

A sound jarred him from his thoughts and he looked toward his window. There it was again. A light, cracking noise. He went to take a look, pulled the drapes back, and raised the yellowing shade. A torrent of reactions engulfed him with such speed that he couldn't grab on to one solidly enough to feel anything. He swayed, clutched the drapes for support. His plan, his neatly laid-out chess game had failed. He looked down at the beach that extended behind the house. Beneath his window, Ham Arnold smiled up at him. He tossed a last pebble at Alden's ghost-white face behind the glass and strolled off toward the boardwalk.

Alden seethed. He stood rooted to the floor watching Ham's receding figure taunt him. He remained immobile for minutes, watching until that figure was nothing more than a speck. He pulled himself from his trance and paced furiously the length of the room. He looked over again and again at the jigsaw pieces of the face on his wall. It shifted, seemed to smile at him, to tease, tormenting his created perfection with edges of disorder. He moved closer. No. It was stagnant. Unchanged.

But there was something more to this subject than his distilled image. He was getting to Alden, eroding his balance, undermining his carefully calculated design. He was playing with Alden, dangling him over that pit again, threatening to submerge him in the swamp of chaos and anarchy. In his mind Alden transformed him into the poisonous witch of his youth, turning the salt-and-pepper waves into the raven Medusa curls of his mother, the broad, strapping chest into the suffocating breasts of that she-beast who smothered him. Alden must be stronger than this adversary. He must plot, engineer, and enact his course of action without distraction—without error. He must correct more than the distillation of the man on pure white paper. He must correct the flesh itself.

Both Alison and James thought that Hamilton Arnold's plan was insane. James felt it might backfire and cost the older man his life. Of course, if it succeeded, there would be reflected glory for him as well. Alison checked on Beth and Maud almost hourly during the fitful night and carefully loaded her nightly companion, the steely black gun.

Sitting in his car across the street and slightly down the block from the Sommers' house, Ham was not quite sure just when he had begun to recognize the possibility that by attaching himself so obviously to this ready-made surrogate family he had also become a very attractive target. As much as he shunned the overt verbosity of psychiatric jargon, he was smart enough to know that a man like Alden Smith could only be pushed so far before he would retaliate. And his kind of retaliation was one which Ham wanted to be well prepared for.

He trusted in his plan and knew that the safety measures he had taken were more than adequate but was still somewhat chagrined at the thought of the clearly frazzled James as his only source of backup. Still, his unfailing instinct told him that if James was going to really crack, it wouldn't be until whatever was going to happen was over. On the plus side, too, was the levelheaded Alison, weighed down now by the burdensome task of balancing her children's safety against her husband's faltering ego and at the same time trying to stay alert to the danger without. Still, she was a strong, competent woman who, Ham believed, would come through it all unscarred. The calmness with which she had accepted Hamilton's involvement in her life (because it was James's choice) while letting him know she disapproved and would hold him accountable, told him right off that she was his kind of person.

Still, he thought to himself as he poured hot coffee from the thermos Alison had given him, the most any of them could do at this point was speculate as to what Alden Smith's plan of action—if he even had one—would be. Ham had theorized to James and Alison that this psychopath had taken the obvious resemblance between his murdered wife and children and Alison and the girls and had carried it to the point where he now completely believed that they were one and the same. Thinking thus, and having blocked out any memory of the crime, he was now courting them, in a way; trying to win them back from the man he saw as his replacement. He sent the postcards, not so much to frighten them but to seduce them. And, Ham had told them, if this was the case, there was no real physical danger to any of them. James and Alison agreed.

What Ham had omitted from his scenario of Alden's motivation was his very solid belief that Smith not only recalled the murders but, through some deviance caused by his particular psychosis, believed that his family had survived them and was going to make sure he did it right this time around. There had been no reason to terrify the Sommers with this truer version of Ham's thoughts on Alden, just as there had been no need to tell them about his own personal involvement with them. If it all worked out—if they all survived—

185

there would be time enough to rehash and analyze what they did right and what might have been done differently. If it turned out the other way, it wouldn't much matter.

It was barely a whisper that Ham heard, not nearly the sound of a car door opening or a movement in the rear car seat, but he felt those hairs on the back of his neck rise and in the instant between making the decision to look over his shoulder and taking the action the blow came and the blade slipped into his body from the seat behind him. Ham felt his body tilt, then slide forward, and suddenly crash with force into the steering wheel, his forehead bruising the cold metal.

James approached the still figure in the car with a mixture of adrenaline-invoked apprehension and fear. He pulled the door open and reached for Ham's shoulder, calling to him to ask why he was positioned so and to awaken him if he had dozed off, when his eye caught sight of the knife plunged halfway into Hamilton's back. He started to reach out to check his pulse but something distracted him, a piece of paper clinging to the sticky, red ooze that ran down Ham's back and onto the car seat. James bent over Ham's body and looked. What he saw made him reel and spin with sickening velocity. He steadied himself on the edge of the car door, fighting to hold down the contents of his churning stomach. Holding a hand tightly over his mouth, he leaned closer, looked again. A postcard, soaked now in Ham's blood, the blade splitting the horrifying image with harrowing symmetry: the faces of Alison, Beth, and Maud.

His whole body churning, James grasped Hamilton's shoulder for support as he tried to steady himself enough to return to the house. He felt the other man's body giving way slightly under his weight. "Don't move me . . ." The words swelled the deathly silent car with sound and made James's heart stop as Hamilton went on. "Just make that call . . . everything else is all set up." His voice breathless and pained.

"God, I thought you were dead!" James felt cold and tingly all over as if he actually was talking to a dead man.

"Let's just hope that's what he thinks."

Chapter 12

IT had been a small mistake, really, not counting on the knife slipping through the protective vest, but still Ham berated himself for not selecting the heavier, more sturdy version. His plan did not allow for injuries, and while his was fortunately little more than a flesh wound in spite of the blood, it hurt like hell. Good thing Alden hadn't used a meat cleaver, his weapon of choice, Ham mused to himself while being patched up, but that was reserved for women and children. Still, despite the stab wound and warnings that he should take it easy for a few days, he was determined to see his plan through to the end—even more so now that he felt certain Alden believed him to be dead.

There was no way of telling for certain just how much of the events of the twenty-four hours following the stabbing of Hamilton Arnold that Alden Smith had seen, but all the participants in the plan behaved in every way as if Ham had been killed. James had managed to pull himself together enough to make the prearranged call to Ham's friend in the police department and the ambulance that arrived a few minutes later removed Ham directly from the car on to a gurney and drove straight from James's house to the morgue. James had alerted Ham's friend to the kind of injury Ham had suffered and one of the ambulance crew had treated the wound behind the covered windows of the van as it drove to the morgue. It was one of the more memorable events in Ham's life, that night spent on a narrow slab in a room full of dead bodies, but it was necessary, he argued, to maintain the charade to the fullest. It was damn hard, too, lying perfectly still beneath the covering of a white sheet while the bandage on his back did little more than protect the area from further injury. He had refused medication, knowing it would cloud his judgment, and he rationalized his pain away with searing thoughts of the torment Alden's victims had gone through. If his plan succeeded, it would all have been worth it.

Getting back into the Sommers' house without being detected took even more careful thought and Ham's eventual scheme was one of his most ingenious. Shortly after eight the next morning, a delivery truck pulled up in front of the Sommers' house and two men carried a large, rolled, and wrapped Oriental rug in through the garage entrance. They only stayed a few minutes, just long enough to put the unopened rug in the middle of the basement floor, receive a tip, and depart. It took James and Alison only a few minutes more to unroll the carpet and free Hamilton Arnold from his cocoon.

With both Maud and Beth safely at school, there was ample time to make Hamilton comfortable in the basement playroom and to provide him with a good breakfast and a bottle of scotch for the long afternoon ahead. He was still in a good deal of pain from the stab wound and Alison fixed a makeshift bed on the couch and brought an assortment of supplies from the upstairs bathroom in case he should need them. He selected two aspirin tablets, swallowed them with some fresh orange juice, and ate the bacon and eggs Alison served him while going over the second half of his plan to catch Alden Smith. Everything hinged on Alden's unquestioning acceptance of Ham's death and there was no doubt in the wily reporter's mind that every move since the stabbing occurred had been carefully chronicled by Smith. Ham was absolutely certain that Alden would now make his final move.

Alison went through the day a reluctant and very vulnerable bystander in her own home. She was told to behave normally, conducting her regular errands without interruption, and her efforts to have Beth and Maud spend the night at a friend's house were strongly vetoed. The slightest change in the daily lives of the members of the Sommers family would tip the scales dangerously in favor of the watching menace that had been stalking them. As long as she played her part perfectly, James and Hamilton assured her, nothing could go wrong. James drove to work and then returned several hours earlier than usual feigning illness, and there was even a delivery from the local pharmacy—some cold tablets—to complete the charade. On the surface it seemed as if every base had been touched and nothing, indeed, could go wrong. But then, there was a virtual stranger camped out in Alison's basement with a jagged cut in his back to prove that no plan is foolproof.

She didn't know what bothered her most, waiting for the interminable day to come to an end or dreading what would happen as soon as evening fell. Sandwiches and coffee were packed in a small picnic basket and a separate bag of food and a thermos was provided for Ham, who would have to stay out of sight. As soon as the sun went down, the two men sneaked out of the house through the garage entrance and James climbed into the driver's seat of his car while Ham crawled into the back and curled up uncomfortably on the floor, where he could not be seen. Safely propped up with his head against the door and a blanket to keep him warm, Ham signaled that all was ready and James backed the car out of the driveway and pulled it out into the street. He drove only a few yards from the house, parked, turned the lights and motor off, and settled back to wait. It was seven P.M.

Four hours later Ham was beginning to think that he might never reach his full height again. Parts of him hurt that he previously didn't know existed and he wished he hadn't eaten two sandwiches or had so much coffee. His stomach ached and he had to urinate. On top of that, James refused to keep quiet in spite of repeated warnings that Alden Smith's eyesight could penetrate anything and he would most assuredly wonder why James was sitting and talking to himself. Clearly, the idea was to set James up as a barrier between Alden and the house but that would only work if Alden believed that James was alone. Then, when he made his diversionary move to distract James, Hamilton could surprise him and nab him on the spot. It was all laid out like the clearest blueprints and Ham would have patted himself on the back for the sheer genius of it had it not hurt so much to move.

There was only one thing wrong with the plan, Ham acknowledged when six A.M. rolled around after a completely uneventful night during which he and James had taken turns sleeping thanks to a tiny periscope Ham had fabricated to allow him to keep an eye on the house during his shift, and that was that Alden Smith was nowhere in sight.

Alison was none too pleased to learn that their guest would be with them another night and the entire plan repeated, perhaps several times if necessary, until Alden took the bait. She had gone out on a limb to explain to the girls that James was working on a very important mission with a detective who was helping them trap the man sending the postcards. But now that Ham would likely be with them for a couple of days, it was difficult for her to keep Beth and Maud out of the basement and to curb their natural curiosity. She hated lying to them and felt doubly trapped: by the calculating team in the basement, who had seemingly forgotten that there were two little girls to consider, and by the waiting observer outside, who knew, too well, that they were there.

James had become totally absorbed in this plot with Hamilton to trap Alden Smith and had lost all contact with his children and most with Alison. For four days, ever since Hamilton Arnold had first showed up, he had been enveloped in this game of detective work, and while Alison was pleased to see his ego in a state of repair, she was more than a little worried about what would happen if the plan fell through, or worse, if James was merely being played for a fool and Hamilton turned out to be the hero.

She had wanted just a few moments alone with James to sort these feelings out, to remind him that his daughters needed an explanation directly from their father and not through a substitute but, try though she would, he would not let her in. In part she understood the walls he had put up. After all, every time she had opened her mouth in recent weeks her words were received by him as weapons. But his total commitment to this newcomer in their lives and his unquestioning acceptance of everything Ham said frightened Alison even more than his recent violent outbursts. Like Ham, she too sensed an impending fissure in James's rational, calm exterior and, having felt the brunt lately of his brutal anger, was terrified at what any crack in the surface might emit from deep within. Trapped thus by these literal and figurative strangers in her life and further hemmed in by her own sense of loyalty and love for her two children and for James, she could only watch and wait.

Night two proved to be a duplicate of the first. Ham drank less coffee this time out and made a pillow out of his jacket which comforted his neck somewhat, but it was a boring wait and an uneventful watch. Both James and Ham were glad they had listened to Alison, who had pointed out that it was very unlikely that Alden Smith would make a move early in the evening while they were all awake. It would make much more sense for James to have dinner with the family and take up his vigil later—around eleven—when the girls went to sleep. It had been a much shorter night all around, that way, and Ham had rested a few extra hours on the couch in the basement instead of the bumpy back floor of James's car.

Something was different about the third night. They all sensed it, felt it creeping around them like a shadow, but it was so intangible as to be barely a breath and none of them mentioned it. Preparations went on as before with Ham crawling into the back of the car with a sandwich and thermos of coffee and James getting into the front seat with his own thermos and a blanket to wrap around his shoulders to ward off the fall chill. The car pulled out of the driveway just after eleven and moved to its regular spot a few doors away while Alison went around the house locking the doors and turning out the lights. Maud had her bubble bath and Beth her shower, homework was proofread and packed away for tomorrow, and fresh pajamas laid out on the beds. Tucked safely in their beds, Beth and Maud secured a promise from Alison to return and say good night after her bath.

Fighting an urge to peek through the blinds and check the street in front of the house, Alison went to her bathroom and turned the water on in the tub. She went back to the bedroom, undressed, slipped a quilted robe over her body, and sat down at her bureau to comb her hair and pin it up for the bath.

"Ma?" Maud's voice had the tentative quality children get when angling for a few extra minutes before bed. She hung back in the doorway to her parents' room waiting for a reaction.

"What's wrong, Maud? It's eleven-thirty, you have school tomorrow, you know."

"I can't sleep. Can I stay up with you a little while?"

"You've only been in bed five minutes so how do you know you can't sleep?" Alison knew the little girl would be exhausted in the morning if she didn't go to bed but was torn between her own desire for company and her motherly duty. She held out her arms and Maud padded over on her soft slippers and cuddled. Alison closed her eyes, thinking how much this ten-year-old still reminded her of the infant and toddler she was just a short time ago. Alison rested her chin on Maud's head and saw that the youngster's eyes were barely open. Smiling, herself now comforted and relaxed, she scooped Maud up in her arms and carried her back to bed,

Outside in the cold, dark car James napped while Ham kept watch with his small periscope and balanced a cup of hot coffee on his stomach. It was a little after midnight and he would wake James at two to begin his shift. There were still lights on in the Sommers' house and the street was empty except for a lone man walking a large, shaggy dog. Still, Ham couldn't shake that sensation that they weren't alone.

Alison hung her robe on the back of the bathroom door and felt the velvety touch of warm bathwater as she slid her body into the tub, rested her head on the lip at one end, and closed her eyes. Soft music wafted from a radio on the sink cabinet a few feet away and her thoughts drifted from one past pleasant memory to another, deliberately—for these few private moments—avoiding any contact with the present. The house was very quiet now that both girls were asleep and the gentle music kept her company and toned down that apprehensive feeling she still had that she was being watched.

"He's doing this on purpose!" Ham said out loud as he tried in vain to make his aching body just a little

194

more comfortable on the floor of the car. He was certain that Alden was taking great sadistic pleasure in drawing every last drop of tension from the past few nights even as he knew that there was no way Alden could know that Ham was still alive. He hated to admit it, but he believed that Alden was now focusing attention on James as an adversary and was biding his time so as to weaken and tire the enemy before striking. Little could he know about the hidden trump card in the backseat. Yet as long as Alden held back his final move, all they could do was hurry up and wait.

Alison was deliciously tired and softly refreshed by the luxurious bath and couldn't wait to snuggle into her bed and erase another day of waiting from her mind. She slipped on a soft, cotton nightgown, let her hair down and brushed it a few strokes, and, thoroughly tempted by the sight of the big, warm bed, climbed inside and pulled the covers up to her chin. She reached over to turn the light out on the night table and suddenly remembered her promise. Almost seduced enough by the sheets to let it pass, she fought sleep for a few more minutes, got out of bed, slipped her bathrobe on over her nightgown, and went to check on the girls.

James awoke an hour before his shift was due and told a grateful Hamilton that he could relax the periscope and take a nap earlier than expected because James was quite alert and not the least bit sleepy. Before he had a chance to pour a cup of hot coffee for himself, the sounds of exhausted snoring drifted from the back of the car. He sipped his coffee, stretched as much as the small space would allow, and looked up and down the barren street carefully. The sensation he had experienced earlier that tonight would be the night was now beginning to fade and he rejected the slightly lingering feeling that he was being secretly observed with assurances to himself that he was merely letting the circumstances of spending three full nights sitting in a car make him paranoid.

Beth and Maud were deep in slumber when Alison closed the door gently to the edge and walked down the hall to her bedroom, finally, to get some sleep. At the last minute she decided to leave the bathroom light on in case James should decide to come in before dawn so that he wouldn't wake her with his stumbling around in the dark. She tossed her robe on the foot of the bed, climbed back in, and turned the light on the night table off. In a few moments she was fast asleep.

Gentle snores still filled the car as Ham slept quite soundly despite the discomfort of his hiding place. James's head was tilted back toward the headrest and his arms and shoulders were loose and relaxed. He, too, was asleep.

Alden Smith stepped out from the cozy niche he had shaped for himself in a hedge across the street from the Sommers' house and looked up and down the silent street. That car was still there, its occupant hoping to trap him these past few nights, but now, worn and tired from the endless wait, harmlessly asleep at the wheel. Alden turned his thoughts to the house, blocked the memory of that car from his mind. Tonight it would all culminate for him, the whole, awful four years of torment, the creative imprisonment, the sense of failure and self-hatred. It would all be over tonight. He would make it right and then he would let it go. He walked slowly toward the house.

A cold chill passed over Alison and she awakened with a start, shivering under the sheet and heavy quilt. She sat up in bed and looked around the room, lightly illuminated by the glow from the bathroom light. She started to slide back under the covers but paused a moment, reached over to the night table, and pulled the top drawer out a few inches so that she could slip her hand inside and slide the gun out from its resting place. For a second or two she sat up in bed holding it in both hands, feeling the sense of security it imparted, then, sleep returning, she placed it on the nightstand within reach and lay down, pulling the covers up to her chin.

Alden stood directly in front of the house, waiving caution for the first time since he knew of this place. The man was asleep in the car. He knew that. The downstairs was dark; the woman and little girls must be upstairs. He walked around to the back of the house, brazenly using the driveway instead of the bramble-filled hedge path. The upstairs, also, was dark. They had gone to bed. He set his bag on the lawn, viewed the second story calmly. He began a slow chant of numbers under his breath to calm his pulse.

Beth turned over in bed and woke up just enough to check on Maud and make certain the little girl was sleeping soundly and was well covered. She thought about making a trip to the bathroom in the hall but decided it was too far and she was too tired. She turned over on her other side and went back to sleep.

"One . . . two . . . three . . . four . . . five . . . six . . . seven . . . one . . . two . . . three . . . four . . . five . . . six . . . seven . . . Alden counted the row of brick steps that led to a back door. He squatted on his heels and watched the upstairs for life. It was almost 3 A.M., he guessed. They were most definitely asleep.

James slept undisturbed in the front seat of the car as Ham dozed on the floor in the back. The blanket had slid off James's shoulders and, without waking, his body followed it down to the soft car seat where he

197

rested his head and fell into a deeper sleep, his frame angled almost ninety degrees with his legs on the floor and his upper body on the front seat.

Alden turned the back doorknob gently. Locked. He tested the dead bolt with his weight. It was bolted. The front door was also locked, he was sure of that. He tried again at the rear entrance, decided next on the kitchen window.

Alison turned on her side in bed, reached instinctively for James, and awakened just for a moment when her hand found cool emptiness. In a second she remembered; he was outside, sitting in the cold car, guarding the house, protecting them. She fell back asleep.

In the driveway, his knapsack over his shoulder, Alden tested the kitchen window. It slid open at his touch. He sprang upward, hoisted himself over the sill, and landed softly in the kitchen sink. He plopped quietly to the floor, balanced his bag on his back.

Hamilton Arnold had almost forgotten where he was, so deep was his sleep. He started to turn over and felt a jab of pain in his back where the knife had entered. He lay still. Looked at his watch and saw that he had another hour to sleep before switching shifts with James. Thank God he was being quiet at last. Ham closed his eyes again and tried to get comfortable.

In the kitchen, Alden formed a tense, white-knuckled fist with his right hand, began the rhythmic, calming beat on his right thigh as he walked to the back door, opened both locks. He selected the gleaming meat cleaver from the butcher-block knife holder on the counter and headed across the room, down the hall, and toward the staircase.

* * *

Maud and Beth each slept curled in little balls beneath their warm covers. Alison lay almost exactly in the middle of the big, lonely bed and slept deeply on her back, covers still pulled up over her chin. The plaid blanket cushioned James as he dozed on the front seat of the car. In back, Ham slept fitfully now, unable to find a comfortable position.

Alden was on the landing. He studied the closed bedroom doors trying to determine which was the master bedroom. It had to be the larger, front-facing one. He had photographed the little girl in the other room whose windows faced both front and side, he recalled. He faced the door of the master bedroom and turned the handle silently.

If it had been possible to toss and turn in that cramped, bumpy, rough-surfaced space, Ham would have managed it that night. He tried to calm himself back to sleep with thoughts of finally capturing Alden Smith but everything hurt too much and he was too restless. He opened his eyes, stared at the inside of the roof of the car, closed them again. Maybe if he just stayed still, he would fall back asleep.

Alden stood motionless at the foot of the large bed. A sleeping body lay almost in its center, oblivious to his presence. He unzipped his bag and very, very quietly removed a tripod; set it up just in front of where she lay. She slept on. He placed his camera in the groove on top of the stand and hooked on the full bulk loader. He set the camera to "automatic." He was pacing himself now, slow and steady, counting to keep his pulse low, avoiding extra movement and extraneous thought. He would achieve perfection this time. This time they wouldn't get away. He picked his bag up and quietly left to repeat the procedure in the children's room down the hall.

* * *

It was damn quiet in the car, Hamilton thought, having given up on sleep, too damn quiet for James to be anything but asleep. A shot of panic ran through Ham's body as he took a chance on being seen and raised himself up off the floor to check the front seat. Sure enough, James was out cold. Ham reached over to shake him when a slight movement—nothing more than a shadow—caught his attention in the corner window that belonged to the two little girls' room. He looked closely. There was definitely movement. He shook James violently.

Having set up a tripod and camera in the children's room and allowing for the necessary alterations that arose from having both girls in two separate beds in the same room, Alden stood again at the foot of the king-sized master bed and gazed solemnly at the sleeping Alison, seeing instead the sleeping form of his wife, Anise. This time . . . he struggled not to speak aloud, to awaken her . . . he would make sure there were no mistakes. He crept back to where his bag rested next to the tripod and removed the gleaming, wood-handled object he had taken from the kitchen below.

There it was again—that stealthy shadow—now in Alison's room, hovering. Ham bolting out of the car, a befuddled James staggering after him, drugged by sleep. Racing toward the house, fumbling keys. Inside. Dashing upstairs, tripping. Racing.

Alden lifted his right hand above the sleeping woman in the bed. The sharp, clean blade of the meat cleaver caught the edge of moonlight that slipped under the window shade and glinted in a deadly angle across her face. The distraction of the light from the bathroom, pushed out of his mind. He struggled as a persistent image crawled into his brain and he was faced with the mayhem of the first time. He fought it

200

off. This time he wouldn't miss that first stroke. She would have no chance to wake and to scream and to escape. A torrent of bloody images flickered across his brain at lightning speed. Bodies, blood, bodies, blood. Yet here she lay and he knew, despite the gory images, that he had missed the first time and now was his chance to correct the disarray. His arm drew back, ready to strike.

"I've got you, you son of a bitch." Ham crashed into the room a step ahead of James, who screamed to Alison as Alden froze, arm poised. Alison groped her way out of sleep, opened a glazed eye, then both. She sat up screaming. Alden could not stir. A fraction's motion could mean death for Alison if that blade fell, and both Ham and James stopped in their tracks. Alison stuffed her hand into her mouth, choked back her screams, thoughts of her two little girls flooding her mind and pushing back her own fear.

Suddenly, the sound of the automatic timer on the camera. The room filled with ominous clicks. Alden panicked. His arm wavering. A quick glance by Alison toward the gun. Alden following. A flash. The cleaver dropped to the floor. Distraction. Alden lunged. Diving for the gun. Ham and James knocked backward by the force of his body. A hand. Quick extension. Like a rattlesnake. The gun, taken. Speed. A blurring exit. Running down the hall, the staircase. Ham on his feet, ordering James to stay with his wife. Flying in pursuit.

Stunned by what he instantaneously perceived as total rejection by his comrade, the ultimate betrayal of one warrior against another, humiliation, James sank to the bedroom floor as if struck by a penetrating wound. Alison weeping, loud moans, her arms held out to him to comfort, be comforted. The sound of her voice grabbing at him, tearing at the sores inflicted by Ham's abandonment, ripping into his brain. Rising to his feet, staring at her tear-soaked face, her wide frightened eyes, the extended pleading arms, her body made fragile by the enveloping bed. She started to crawl toward him, reaching. He backed away. Cornered. Helpless in the face of those cries. His destruction. The clicking. Timed, balanced, careful shots. Salvation. He turned toward the source. Tore it from its tri-legged resting place and aimed it at her face. Released the auto-shutter. A surge of power. Force. The control in his hands. Aiming, placing, framing, shooting. Her terrified face. Her begging arms. The tears. The fright. Ecstasy.

The slam of the door opening. Two screaming little girls, white, paper-thin skin, bright red mouths, tear-dripping eyes. Tiny hands. Pounding him. Grabbing at his legs. Screeching. Alison now up close. Her hand on the lens. All three against him. Ripping it from his hands. Thrown to the floor. Thrashing. The four of them now on the bed, struggling. Twined together, the quilt binding them. Salty moisture. Tears, running noses, saliva. The din of pleading, screaming voices.

Quiet. In his head. Over. He was watching them, the scene of panic. An observer. Seeing himself tumbling on the bed, grappling with this woman, those children. That strange man, much like him. A sudden stinging welt. His face sore. Returning. Aware. His wife. His children. The mix of his own tears with theirs. Hugging. Caressing. Endless forgiving kisses. Alert. The danger still real. Cleaver on the floor. Gun removed. Alden running. Ham, still injured, pursuing.

"I have to help him." James pulling away from them, untangling arms and legs from the bedclothes and clinging hands. Alison and children huddling, trembling. The sudden loud, powerful "crack" of a shot. James frozen in his place. Silence. Afraid to breathe. A pause. James's hand reaching for the phone, shaking. Dialing. The police.

Alison stood protectively huddled around Beth and Maud in the chilly October night as James and Hamilton watched the police outline the body on the back lawn, lift it to a stretcher, and carry it away. A dark, blackish fluid seeped into the grass and dyed it morbidly. Alison hid the faces of the two girls in her robe.

It was Ham's friend, Captain McCary, who took the statement, removed the gun. There would be questions to answer, forms to fill out but nothing that couldn't wait until morning. It was clearly a suicide. Ham's hands had never touched the gun. At last it was really over. They were safe. Alden Smith's plan had failed. He had achieved his perfection only in death. He had done it with one shot.

Chapter 13

A MONTH'S healing time brought the family back
to a regular pace, a normal existence. The two
girls even gathered their courage to go trick-or-treating
on Halloween, with Alison as chaperon. Maud got to
wear Beth's old softball uniform and there wasn't even
an argument. James resumed work right away, the
five-day sick leave written off as due to a bad cold.
What had started as an uneasy acceptance of Ham
Arnold now felt quite normal and comfortable. The
children had taken to him immediately and without
question, and using their infallible instincts as a guide,
Alison and James had followed. The stabbing of Hamilton and the death of Alden had canceled each other
out. One wound had healed slowly and left a small
scar. The other, gaping forever wide in their memories, could not be healed. Time, once a destructive
invader in their lives, became a friend.

Normal mail delivery was arranged and the post
office box was canceled. Postcards were a thing of the
past and they were even able to laugh when a friend of
James's dropped them one from Paris and they reacted
with startled amusement to the pleasant photo on the
front, the lack of detailed artistry in the workmanship.
They much preferred it that way and the card stayed
on the mantel piece. Though everyone else thought
they had long since been burned, James had secretly

kept the other cards as a perverse reminder to himself of what they had been through. Even privately he could not clearly define his motivation. He just knew he needed them.

He had also continued to use his 35mm camera quite regularly, though no longer with the violent obsessiveness of the past. There were now photos of a smiling Ham Arnold mingled with the family shots in the bulging album and James was thinking of buying another book to fill with the many prints he knew he would have in the future. He even toyed with the idea of taking a refresher course in photo developing and installing a small darkroom in the basement when he added up the cost of sending each roll of newly shot film out to be processed. Alison kept her opinion to herself. Privately, too, Ham Arnold made a note to keep an extra sharp eye on James. Instinct and a long history had taught him to be most wary of the eye of the storm, where it was always most deceptively quiet.

Part of the recovery plan had included fresh landscaping of the backyard. A large section of lawn where Alden's body had fallen, facedown in the grass, blood pouring from a hole in his skull, was now paved over in white concrete, neatly patterned in large, clean, uneven squares. A barbecue had also been built and the shape of the lawn resculpted to eradicate any trace of the past. A bright yellow umbrella table would decorate the new patio in the spring and the yard looked new, fresh, and most of all safe. Even the impressionable Maud felt free to romp there and to sit with her dolls on the new, hard surface.

The arrival of the day's mail no longer sent chills down Alison's spine and Maud and Beth had long since resumed their alternate chore of mail deliverers. In that marvelous way of children's minds, they had put the past events to rest and thought nothing of racing to the corner to greet the mailman, plunging anxious hands into the steel box next to the front door and making the rounds to each parent with his or her mail. Once in a while, there was even something addressed to one of them.

All in all, things were quite back to normal and the addition of Ham Arnold as a kind of benevolent family watchdog—he had that gruff, tumbly air about him always—was quite pleasant, even for the sensitive James. On those days or weekends when Ham drove over from Oceanview there was always a special feeling to the house as if a long-missed uncle had come to town. He had never told them his very private reasons for helping them, for wanting so desperately to vanquish Alden Smith, and they had continued to respect his wishes by not asking. But somehow, each one of them knew that they were connected to him by something a lot more binding than chance.

The arrival of an overstuffed envelope of freshly developed photos was practically a weekly event since James's passion turned into a habit. It became Maud's personal, self-assigned task to open and review each shot before submitting them to her overly critical father, who rarely liked his own work. This particular Friday was no exception and she handed the rest of the mail unceremoniously over to her older sister to deliver while sitting down Indian-style on the foyer floor to look through the latest batch of photos. Beth carried the other mail to her breakfasting parents.

A knock on the back door told them Ham had arrived in time for coffee and Beth let him in after eliciting a promise that he would attend the softball game on Sunday. He poured himself a cup of black French roast and joined James and Alison at the table while Beth neatly peeled an orange over the sink.

Suddenly, coffee and toast were interrupted by a banshee wail from Maud. They all raced to the front hall to find her cowering over a sloppy pile of photographs, tears streaming down her face and her body quivering in terror. Alison held her while James and Ham dropped to their knees and searched through the pile, hearts pounding. There it was. Different from the others, slightly larger, the white border thicker, more defined. Mixed in with smiling family photos of pleasant memories. James reached for it, intercepted by Ham. A strong hand covering the square of paper. Waiting. Faces tense. Ham took the card, stood, holding it close to him, not looking. James on his feet as well, hand extended, his pride irritated. Ham still held on to the rectangular slice of paper, those little hairs on the back of his neck beginning to rise. A postcard. No one moved.

"This is ridiculous. What are we all so frightened of, the man's dead!" James tried to take the card from Ham. Failed. His hand fell back to his side. "Come on, Ham . . . guys . . . it's a mistake . . . it has to be. Someone read about us in the paper and decided to scare us. That's all. It got mixed up in the pictures by mistake. Believe me, it's nothing!" He struggled to convince the others but his trembling voice betrayed him. The photo envelope had been sealed at the processing shop. It was mailed directly to the house. The gummed seal had not been opened before Maud touched it. But still, there had to be a logical explanation. Why didn't someone say something? He looked at Ham. Surely he wasn't afraid to look, to acknowledge the fact that it must be some kind of sick joke. James waited.

Slowly, inching the card away from his chest, Ham glanced down slightly to observe the image. Tiny drops of sweat formed on his temples and tight, white lines formed around his mouth. His knuckles tightened. He swallowed hard, passed the card to James. Alison watched as her husband's shoulders tensed and a ripple of nervous movement ran through his upper body. She tried to move toward him but Beth and Maud clung to her and held her back. She waited, terrified to ask. Ham placed a solid hand on her shoulder, waiting.

James stared down at the card in speechless horror, color drained from his face, sensation from his flesh. Then he felt it. A chilling ripple; a creeping, crawling movement that began at the base of each nerve and rode a crest to the surface of his body. He shivered. It was impossible. It was a trick. A ghoulish prank. It was also real.

The card was cleanly printed, carefully blocked and balanced—perfectly planned. The style was unmistakable. As was the image. There, faceup on the brand-new, spanking concrete patio in the Sommers' yard, a dark stream of blood pouring from a black hole in his brain, blank, expressionless, dull eyes staring wide at the numb James, was Alden Smith.

The girls inched Alison closer to James, fighting the protective strength of Hamilton, their fear momentarily overcome by curiosity. He held the card gingerly, instinct telling him to hide it from them but reflexes lacking. Stone-faced, Alison drew a trembling hand to her mouth, pressed closer to James. A fevered storm of screams, gasps from Beth and Maud. Hamilton trying to envelop them all in his strong, shielding arms. All eyes riveted to that impossibly tangible image. Compelled somehow, James flipped the card over. Then they saw it. There. On the back of the card for the first time. A message. Darkly scrawled across the clean, white paper untouched by postmark or stamp, the words:

"Wish You Were Here"